CURSE OF ATLANTIS

PLYMOUTH ROCK

M. PAUL HOLLANDER

outskirtspress
DENVER, COLORADO

Outskirts Press, Inc.
http://www.outskirtspress.com

ISBN: 978-1-4787-6630-8

Outskirts Press and the "OP" logo are trademarks belonging to Outskirts Press, Inc.

PRINTED IN THE UNITED STATES OF AMERICA

To my daughter, Chelsea

Our rides together

are some of my fondest memories.

Acknowledgements

Dawn Stone

Editor

Cover Art

Jessica (Kirsenlohr) Landon

Plymouth, Massachusetts

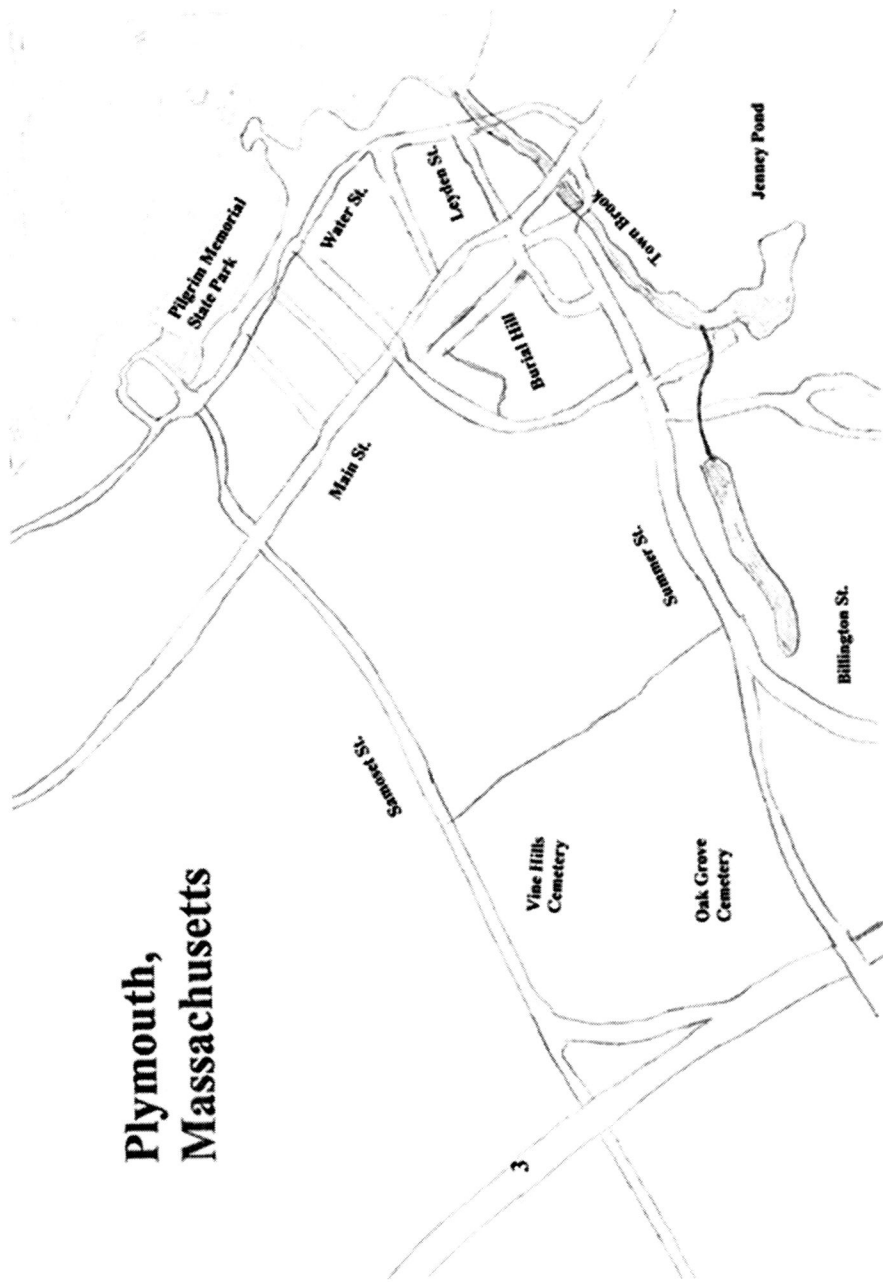

Pilgrim Memorial State Park

Water St.

Leyden St.

Town Brook

Jenney Pond

Burial Hill

Main St.

Summer St.

Billington St.

Samoset St.

Vine Hills Cemetery

Oak Grove Cemetery

3

Prologue

"LORI SAMPSON," CALLED the principal.

There was some polite applause, along with a couple of wolf whistles and nervous laughter.

"Debra Sandaval," the principal continued, unfazed by the antics of some of the large crowd gathered in the auditorium.

More polite applause.

"Almost done," thought Harley bitterly. "High school has been the worst four years of my life. God, please make the next four a little better."

Harley was standing at the base of the steps that led up to the stage, where his school's principal was calling the names of his classmates. Most he knew, but only being at this high school for his junior and senior year, there were quite a few he did not recognize at all.

"Probably a good thing I don't know them. They'd probably end up dead, especially if I cared for them at all."

That thought began for Harley a quick recollection of all that had occurred to him in the previous four years. He shook his head at the images his mind evoked.

Harley had been born and raised in central Wisconsin, and during the summer between 8th and 9th grade, Jen, his mother, had died on a trip to North Carolina. What had been thought of as just a tragic motorcycle accident had turned out to be something much more sinister.

The following summer, Dave, his father, decided to do some private investigating himself. He had told Harley that Jen had made an accidental discovery at a place called Roanoke Island. Harley had finagled his way into going along, as he wanted to know the truth about his mother's death.

In that summer between his freshman and sophomore year, Harley had ridden on the back of his dad's big Harley-Davidson all the way from Wisconsin to the Outer Banks, where they camped at the local Triple C, which was short for Campgrounds 'Cross the Country. His dad had a pull-behind trailer that became a pop up camper once it was set up at whatever location he chose. In that way, they could always have a base camp, and day trips could vector in any direction.

It was at this particular campground situated on the ocean that Harley had met Anna, a young girl his own age. They became close very quickly, and as Harley began to hear her story, he realized that his mother's death mirrored what had occurred to Jeff, Anna's father, two years earlier. Her father had been killed on his motorcycle under mysterious circumstances as well.

In a twist of fate, Anna's mom Marlene was being extorted by Jack, a man who had been friends with Anna's dad. Jack had threatened to harm Anna if Marlene did not do as he said. Jack was after a piece of an old journal that Harley's mom had found at Roanoke. The journal page stated that an amulet from the legendary Atlantis existed, and it had been hidden at Roanoke by the early colonists, particularly Thomas Hariot, John White, and Sir Francis Drake.

Two years earlier Jack actually had found the nine piece amulet, except for the center piece. Anna's dad had found the missing center piece earlier, and had unknowingly given it to Anna as a souvenir for her rock collection. Jack had not known of this exchange, and thinking Jeff had the amulet piece on his person, had run Jeff off the road and killed him. He had searched the body but came away empty.

The following year, Jack had seen Jen pick up a journal page. He knew he needed both the amulet and journal together to prove the existence of Atlantis-and to make himself rich.

Marlene never knew her husband had given her daughter the missing piece, and as she manipulated the situation by inviting Harley and his dad over for dinner one night, she was unaware that her daughter was going to show Harley the missing piece from the valuable amulet.

It became a race against time, and fate intervened. A meeting between the four of them at the Lost Colony of Roanoke was interrupted by Jack, who had been keeping a close eye on Marlene. There was a heated exchange, and Jack had shot Marlene, Anna, and Dave. Then he forced Harley to take him to their campground and give him the missing journal piece. He also figured out that Anna had the missing amulet piece, so they had to return to the Lost Colony to retrieve it.

In a fit of rage, Harley, who had been forced to drive, ran the truck directly into the wall of a building, which hurtled Jack, who was not wearing a seat belt, into the windshield, killing him instantly. Harley, who had on his seat belt, was able to scramble out and return to the spot where the shooting had taken place.

Unfortunately, Anna and Marlene had suffered mortal wounds, and Harley's dad had barely survived. His short-lived friendship with the beautiful Anna was over, leaving Harley a hurt and bewildered young man.

In the meantime, the discovery of the journal and amulet was made public, and Harley and his father had become celebrities of a sort. However, before he had to give the artifacts to the authorities, Harley had secretly made copies of both of them. On the journal page had been a coordinate in invisible ink, which became visible on the copy due to some chemical reaction. He and his father determined the location as Jamestown, the first permanent English colony.

That had been all the investigating for that particular summer.

Strange occurrences then began to plague the two. Sickness and injuries prevented them from traveling to Jamestown until the following summer between Harley's sophomore and junior years. He had turned 16, so his present from his father had been a brand new Harley-Davidson Street Glide. On this trip, each would ride solo, with his dad pulling the trailer behind him.

The two bikers had made a stop on the way to Jamestown in order to visit the graves of Anna and her parents. This was where Harley began to have feelings of being followed. It was also where he began to consider some of the unusual weather that seemed to occur whenever anyone was investigating Atlantis.

At Roanoke, there had been three consecutive hurricanes hitting the Outer Banks over the previous three years. After the first, Anna's dad had died. Following the second storm, Harley's mom had perished. The third storm paralleled the deaths of Anna and Marlene.

Harley and his dad had continued their trip to Jamestown, Williamsburg, and Yorktown-the Historic Triangle- and after visits to the replica of Jamestown and also a stop in Williamsburg, they had returned to Jamestown to tour the original James Fort. It was there, where once again, nature seemed to send them a warning.

A freak tornado, something that had never occurred in Jamestown, had nearly killed them as they toured the Voorhees Archaearium. Harley had somehow been snatched by the tornado and flung out of the building. Miraculously, he had only been knocked unconscious, and when regained consciousness, he was staring at the remains of a skeleton's head, which turned out to be the remains of Captain Bartholomew Gosnold, one of the captains of the three ships that had brought John Smith and the other settlers to the American shores.

In addition, Harley found he was grasping a second amulet, this one in the form of a vortex, and with all the same markings as the first amulet, which had been in the shape of a hurricane. Lying on the ground was a leather parcel that contained a letter from John Smith, indicating that this second amulet was being hidden with the body of Gosnold until it could be recovered by Captain Christopher Newport, who had been the captain of the entire fleet of ships. Newport, who had chosen the site of Jamestown, had also been known as the original Captain Hook because he had lost an arm in a battle earlier in his life.

The connection between Roanoke and Jamestown could not be ignored, and Harley and his dad continued their investigating. After making copies of the letter and amulet, Harley had returned to Jamestown to assist with the cleanup from the tornado. Meanwhile, his father was at Williamsburg, at the William and Mary library, attempting to decipher the clues in the letter.

Harley had a nice surprise waiting for him at Jamestown. Because he had been instrumental in saving a number of people from the wreckage of the tornado, he had been interviewed by the local media. Afterward, however, a policeman, who had at first seemed very helpful, now began to question Harley's motives for being at Jamestown.

This spooked Harley, and when his father showed up at Jamestown, Harley told him of the encounter. His father also had some pertinent information, but he did not want to show it to Harley in a public area. They decided to take their bikes to the other end of Jamestown Island to discuss the findings in private. However, once again, fate intervened, and Harley never found out what his father had desired to tell him.

Those feelings of being followed came true once they pulled over and parked their bikes. As they dismounted, two eerily familiar people pulled up behind them and pulled out handguns. The two were spitting images of Jack and Marlene. Through a quick explanation, Harley found out that they were Jake, Jack's twin brother, and Melanie, Marlene's sister. They were married, former Marines, and were out for revenge, as well as getting their hands on the amulet and letter that Harley had found.

This had all been explained while walking Harley and his dad down a trail to an isolated area where the couple could dispose of Harley and his dad. However, when they realized that the amulet and letter were in Dave's motorcycle, they had to return to the road to retrieve them.

It was there where the shootout occurred. The policeman from Jamestown was, for some reason, hiding in the bushes as they returned. When he called to the couple to give up, the shooting began. Harley and his dad had grasped the opportunity to run, and both jumped on their bikes and sped off. Unfortunately their escape was blocked, and they had to follow the road, which was a loop, right back to where they had been.

They were being chased by Jake, who was in his truck, but Melanie had blocked the road with the policeman's car, and Harley and his dad had been forced to dump their bikes in order to avoid crashing into the automobile. Jake and Melanie took this opportunity to again capture the two bikers and force them to give up the amulet and letter.

Once again, Mother Nature had other plans. A second tornado dropped out of the sky, and the result was catastrophic, both physically and emotionally. Harley again escaped unharmed, but when he searched through the debris he found Melanie's body pierced by a tree limb, and worse, his father impaled by another branch.

His father attempted to tell him something, but all Harley heard was, "They da..." His father died a moment later. Dazed, Harley began to return to the road, only to be stopped by Jake, who was pinned under a fallen tree, but still able to train his gun on Harley. Just as Harley thought he was going to die, a figure appeared between himself and Jake.

The delay caused Jake to finally collapse and die. An artery in his leg had been severed, and he had bled to death. The figure that had saved Harley turned out to be an almost exact replica of Anna. It was, in fact, her cousin Abby, who had actually sent the police officer to stop her parents, and then followed on foot to see what had occurred.

Harley received quite the revelation when Abby shared that she knew all about him. Anna and she had texted continuously the previous summer. Abby had been in Greece with her parents at that time, which explained why Harley had never seen them at Anna's funeral.

Somehow, the police officer had survived the shootout, although he had been injured seriously. After a police investigation, with Harley and Abby being questioned thoroughly, the police chief had told the two that the officer wanted to see them.

The two teens traveled to the hospital to visit, and it was there, where once again, strange events occurred. The police officer's name was Chris Newport, basically the same as the captain of the fleet that came to Jamestown 400 years earlier. In addition, the wounds Chris had received during the shootout with Abby's parents resulted in the amputation of his one arm, making him, in essence, the new Captain Hook.

This was almost too much for the newly orphaned Harley to take. To make matters worse, Chris had been following the Atlantis story all along, and he had overheard the conversation between Abby's parents and Harley and his father. He knew Harley had found something at Jamestown, and Harley felt obligated to share the amulet and letter with him.

The three came to the decision to return the two objects to the proper authorities, and once again Harley was in the limelight. It was not an especially happy occasion. He no longer had possession of the two artifacts, although he did have copies that his father had made.

He also did not know what his father had found in his research.

What Harley did have was a budding relationship with Abby. Both were now orphans, and decisions had to be made. With so much tragedy occurring around them, they found comfort in each other. Very quickly they became attached, and a romance began.

Harley had to make a decision. With whom should he now live? His dad's brother, Uncle Ron, was now his legal guardian. Harley was torn between staying in Wisconsin and moving to Michigan, where his dad's extended family lived, including Harley's grandma.

Finally, he asked his grandma if he could live with her. She readily agreed, and even promised to help him see Abby as often as time permitted. Abby, in the meantime, had moved in with her grandma as well. The distance between Michigan and North Carolina was still vast, but the two grandmas allowed Harley and Abby to fly back and forth occasionally to see each other.

There was also the relationship between the two and Chris, who was recovering nicely in Virginia. The teenagers had the opportunity to visit with him when they returned to Jamestown for a groundbreaking ceremony. A new museum near James Fort was going to replace the destroyed archaearium.

The three decided that they would remain in touch and try to figure out what more could be revealed about Atlantis, and that was where it was left. Then, in a stroke of luck, Harley made a discovery in his father's possessions. In the touring pack was a piece of luggage that his father and mother had used for a number of years. Harley had been told about a secret compartment on the one side of it. His father and mother had used it both for the Roanoke and Jamestown discoveries in order to keep the artifacts safe and hidden.

What Harley discovered was a companion compartment on the opposite side. His father must have discovered it just before he died because inside was a set of notes that his father had made on that fateful day when the second tornado had struck.

It was a chronological list of people and events from Jamestown, and at first Chris, Anna, and Harley could not decipher anything from them. Then, one day when Abby was visiting Harley in Michigan, Harley made a connection. His dad's clues were leading them to the next permanent English colony-Plymouth, Massachusetts, home of the Pilgrims. The two decided to contact Chris and let him know. Then they could make arrangements to meet there and investigate again.

"Maybe it would have been better if I had never found Dad's notes," Harley thought sadly, as he began to climb the steps to the stage and receive his high school diploma.

Plymouth Rock

(A Year Earlier)

━━◄(I)►━━

"GRANDMA, ARE YOU sure I can't go on my bike? I went to Jamestown last year."

"Harley, your uncle and I discussed this. We were more than willing to allow you to replace your motorcycle with the insurance money, but this is not okay. You just turned 17, so we are still responsible for you. I know you are more than capable of riding out East, but last year you also had your father with you. Going alone is just a bad idea."

Harley sighed. He knew Grandma Schultz was being just that-a grandmother- and he loved her for that, but he was equally frustrated that she and Uncle Ron would not let him go to Massachusetts on his own, at least not on his pride and joy, a brand new Harley-Davidson Road Glide. The bike had replaced his Street Glide that had been destroyed in the second tornado at Jamestown.

Grandma Schultz continued, "You may still go, but we want you to fly there. Plus I'm sure Abby's grandma wouldn't be all that enthused about you two gallivanting all over the East Coast alone. The deal is that Officer Newport will meet you two at Boston's airport, and you three can go explore to your hearts' content. Plus, he is able to rent a car there, whereas you two are still too young."

Everything she said made sense, but Harley was still more than a little disappointed. He yearned for the freedom of the road, and leaving his baby covered in the garage was not part of that plan. He had picked her out as soon as the spring thaw had opened up the road for riding in April, and he had been riding for two months now.

His 17th birthday had just been celebrated, the summer between his junior and senior year in high school had just begun, and Abby had flown in for the occasion. He had taken her for a couple of rides throughout the Lower Peninsula, and he was extremely hopeful that they would be able to road trip together. They had discussed the possibility, presented it to Grandma Schultz and Uncle Ron, and it had been vetoed almost immediately.

Now, Abby had returned to her home, and plans were still being made for a trip to Plymouth, but with a chaperone accompanying them. At least the chaperone was Chris, and since he was in on their private investigation, there was much less arguing about taking the bike.

"Okay, Grandma, you win. I'll call Abby and Chris, and we will work out flight plans and whatnot."

"Of course I win, Harley," she poked him. "Was there ever a doubt?"

Harley laughed. Grandma was as funny as she was loving. She was also tough. Very few people would stand up to her when she made up her mind.

Grandma then asked, "What's got you so excited about going to Plymouth, other than seeing your girl again? I mean, she just left here." She grinned at him.

"Cut it out, Grandma," Harley grumbled good-naturedly. She definitely knew how to push his buttons.

"Okay, okay," she relented. "So, what are you three going to do?"

"Well, I really liked learning about Roanoke and Jamestown, despite everything, so I thought the next obvious place to visit was Plymouth Rock since that was the next place settled. Plus there is Gloucester, where they have the shipwreck memorial, and Salem has the witch trials. Plus Boston has Bunker Hill and all the Revolutionary War stuff."

He conveniently left out the Atlantis search, which was the real reason for the trip. Only Chris, Anna, and Harley knew of his dad's notes, and none of them were about to go public until they had a chance to explore themselves. Had he told his family about it, combined with all that had happened previously, they might forbid him to make this journey.

"You are your parents' child, checking out all that history. Well, go make your calls, figure out your plans, and then run them by me. We'll make sure you catch your flight. Go."

Harley stood up and gave her a quick hug and peck on the cheek. "Thanks, Grandma."

———————

The calls were made, plans were established, and in short order Harley found himself boarding a plane at Detroit Metro Airport and heading for Logan International in Boston. It was a two hour flight, and Harley was able to enjoy the freedom of being on his own, albeit minus the rumbling of his bike. "Next year, when I'm 18, I'll be able to head out on my own, right after graduation."

Harley was sitting on the plane, and since it was only partially full, he was able to have a seat by the window, as well as having no one beside him. He stared out the window as the plane roared down the runway and slowly lifted into the air. Once the plane was airborne, Harley decided to again study the notes his father had written on that fateful day just the year before. He glanced around to make sure no one was paying any attention to him, and then he reached into his pocket and pulled out the folded paper that he had examined so many times in the past few months. He stared at it again.

Gosnold
1602 Cape Cod, 1607 Jamestown Dies of malaria

Smith
1607 Jamestown, capture by Powhatan, 1608 saved by Newport, True Relation written, 1609 burned in explosion, goes back to England, 1614 explores New England, 1615 second trip to New England, 1616 meets Pocahontas and John Rolfe in England, writes "A Description of New England", 1620 considered for Mayflower trip, not chosen by Pilgrims, 1624 writes "Generall Historie, 1630 writes "True Travels...", 1631 dies.

Newport
1588 Armada battle, 1590 loses arm, 1592 captures Madre de Deus, 1606 hired by Virginia Company, 1607 Jamestown, chooses location, 1608 First Supply, saves Smith, meets Powhatan, Second Supply in September, 1609–10 Sea Venture (Third Supply) shipwreck in Bermuda, make it to Jamestown after Smith leaves, 1613 joins East India Company, goes to East Indies, 1614 returns to England, 1615 starts second voyage. 1617 dies.

Pocahontas
1607 Smith saved???meeting with Powhatan,1613 captured by English, held for ransom, 1614 marries John Rolfe, 1615 has baby son, 1616 travels to England, meets John Smith again, 1617 dies.

John Rolfe
1609 on Sea Venture, shipwrecks, 1610 makes it to Jamestown, 1611 cultivate tobacco, 1614 married Pocahontas, 1616 travels to England and meets Smith, 1617 wife P. dies, sails back to Jamestown, 1621 appointed to colonial government, 1622 dies

Others on Sea Venture
Sir Thomas Gates, William Strachey, Sir George Somers, Stephen Hopkins

Others at Jamestown
Wingfield, Ratliffe, Martin, Kendall, Captain Archer

Others in England (common interests)
Capt. Jones (Harwich), Drake, John Alden

Greek (Atlantis)
Plato, number/letter relationship, symbolism

Harley was glad he had actually paid attention to his father's history lessons because he, like any other normal teenager, would normally have seen the Jamestown settlement and the Plymouth settlement as two separate entities. However, as he perused the list, not only the names, but also some of the anecdotal notes, he observed that some of the people involved at Jamestown had also been involved, either directly or indirectly, with the famous *Mayflower* and the Pilgrims.

He had explained the connections to Abby, and then they had Skyped with Chris and pointed them out to him. As a police officer, he had, of course, been trained to investigate criminal and/or mysterious events. Chris found all of the connections to be reasonable, and he said he would double check Harley's findings, along with any other information he could dig up. He had then promised to meet them in Plymouth whenever they all could get together. They were a team, and no one individual was going to investigate without the others there. Too much had happened to all three of them to betray one another's trust.

Now, they would all be arriving in Boston within a couple hours of one another. They could rehash what they knew, and then they could proceed to Plymouth and do some exploring. With any luck, something would reveal itself and help them solve the mystery of Atlantis. Harley shuddered once as he thought about that. "Bad luck counts as luck too," he mumbled.

At Roanoke and Jamestown, the revelations were followed shortly thereafter with people's deaths. Not just any people either, but those closest to the others involved. The fact that his dad had narrowly missed being killed at Roanoke, only to die the following year at Jamestown as a result of the tornado, had not gone undetected by Harley.

Now Harley had grown close to Chris, who narrowly escaped death at, almost unbelievably, the hands of Abby's parents. It had cost Chris his arm though, and while Chris held no particular grudge toward Abby, or even her parents for that matter, Harley could not help but worry and wonder what the future held for his newfound friends.

Then there was Abby. Harley's short-lived relationship with her cousin Anna had been one thing, and Harley still had occasional nightmares about that particular incident. Abby, however, was something to behold. As much as Harley had grown attached to Anna in such a short period of time, Abby left him often tongue-tied when she flashed her smile at him. Many times he could not believe that she was actually his, well, girlfriend.

Harley sat back in his seat. *Girlfriend.* That word had a nice ring to it. They had never actually said that they were dating, and the words *boyfriend* and *girlfriend* had never actually crossed their lips, but Harley knew how he felt about Abby, and he was certain she felt the same way. The way she kissed him left no doubt. She was passionate in every aspect of her young life, and Harley now felt very protective of her.

Harley also recalled having spoken with his father about the possibility of a curse, and while his father had not refuted the idea, he had not validated it either. They had agreed that far too many events had occurred to be coincidental. There must be a connection somewhere, somehow.

Then there was the idea that his dad never had the opportunity to actually tell him what he had found. He had written all these notes, but without some sort of verification, there was no way to be 100% sure what he had found was even positive. The thought that he may have found something negative always lingered in the back of Harley's mind.

The pilot came over the loudspeaker, announcing that they soon would be landing, and that all passengers should place their trays in an upright position and prepare for the descent into Boston.

Harley folded up his father's notes, placed them in his pocket, and tightened his safety belt. Going over the notes and thinking about all that had occurred had made the time pass very quickly. His somewhat worried demeanor changed rapidly to one of excitement and anticipation.

True, he had just seen Abby just a couple of weeks earlier, but every day that she was away was more difficult than the previous one. It was a feeling Harley had never felt before, and while bothersome, it also felt good to know that his feelings toward Abby were genuine.

According to their plans, Harley would actually be the last to arrive. Chris and Abby should have arrived already, and they agreed to meet at the baggage claim where Harley would pick up his luggage.

The plane bumped gently onto the runway and coasted along the tarmac until it reached the gate. Everyone began grabbing their carry-ons and heading down the narrow aisle. The flight attendant thanked each passenger as they disembarked, and momentarily Harley found himself in the terminal.

The flight attendant had announced the number of the baggage claim, so Harley quickly looked at the signs above his head and followed them. As he entered the claim area, he heard a familiar female voice shout, "Harley, over here!"

And there she was. She charged right up to him, throwing herself into his arms and wrapping her legs around his waist. "I missed you!" she exclaimed breathlessly, and proceeded to give him a long, gentle kiss.

When she pulled away, Harley noted a man standing behind her, grinning from ear to ear. Chris saluted him, and Harley immediately caught the flash of the hook that now replaced the amputated arm. For a moment, the smile vanished from Harley's face, but Abby's presence overshadowed any pessimistic thoughts.

She pulled on his face, forcing him to look into those dazzling eyes that all but mesmerized Harley. "Didn't you miss me?" she challenged. She purposely stuck out her lower lip in a pout.

"Little birdie is gonna poop on that lip if you stick it out any farther," Harley teased.

Abby glared at him, but he quickly laughed and then said, "Yes, I missed you. More than you know." With that he gently pecked her on the lips, and Abby's alluring smile returned. Harley had a difficult time taking his eyes off her, but he was feeling a bit discourteous toward his other friend.

He gently untangled himself from Abby, approached Chris, and they embraced in a giant bear hug. "Great to see you, Harley!" Chris announced. "You're looking well, and I think you have grown some since I last saw you."

"Some," Harley admitted. "You're looking pretty good yourself. How is everything?"

Chris understood this to be a question about his arm. He nodded, held up his artificial appendage, and laughed, "All is well. Captain Hook is at your service."

Harley shook his head. It was hard for him to believe that Chris could be so nonchalant about his disability. Harley was unsure if he could have handled something that traumatizing nearly as well as Chris. Of course, if Chris was going to make light of it, then Harley was not about to be the killjoy of the group.

"Okay then, Hook, how shall we proceed?"

Chris grinned. "Your luggage should be coming through any second now. The baggage carousel is right over there." He pointed with his hook at the metal contraption just a few yards away.

The trio proceeded over to the carousel, where the luggage was just beginning to appear. Harley quickly claimed his bag, and then turned and said, "What now?"

"I have a car waiting at the rental place, so we just need to shuttle over to it. Let's go."

Each one grabbed their individual bags and exited the terminal. Fortunately, the shuttle arrived momentarily, and soon they were at the rental car facility. Chris went inside to sign for it, while Harley and Abby waited outside.

Abby set her bags down and wrapped her arms around Harley's waist. "I can't believe we get 10 whole days to ourselves. This is going to be so much fun."

"Not quite all to ourselves," Harley corrected, nodding at Chris as he came toward them waving the keys. "Still, this is going to be memorable."

Chris reached them and grabbed his luggage. "Car is over there," he pointed. "Let's go."

"So where are we staying?" Abby asked after they had hopped in the car, and Chris had fired the engine.

"Triple C, over by Plymouth. It's just a hop, skip, and a jump from the town itself, and even closer to Plimoth Plantation. Very convenient for us, if you ask me," Chris finished.

"Grandma Larson said that I was supposed to make sure that I take care of the lodging," Abby stated.

"And Grandma Schultz said I should take care of the food and the cost of any tours we are taking," added Harley, "especially since you told her you would take care of the rental car."

Chris was about to protest, but Abby cut him off. "And don't argue with us about it, or we will sic our grandmas on you."

Chris chortled at that statement. "Okay, then. Deal. Glad I don't have to deal with those scary grandmas on a daily basis." He then became a little more serious. "How are things going with your new living arrangements?"

Abby answered first. "Grandma Larson has been great. Don't get me wrong, I miss my folks, but she has been absolutely fantastic. Not traveling all over the world has been a blessing too. It's nice having stability."

Chris nodded. "Stability is a good thing. How about you, Harley?"

Harley delayed responding for a moment. "Grandma Schultz has been great too, considering I probably turned her life upside down by moving in with her. Sometimes I wonder if I shouldn't have gone to Uncle Ron's or even stayed in Wisconsin."

"I wondered about that," Chris commented. "Do you regret the move, now that you've been there almost a year?"

"No, not really, I mean I used to go and visit my mom's grave a lot, so that's kind of out now, but I suppose I will go visit my other grandma, and then I can visit the old hometown while I'm there. Sometimes I feel like I have abandoned them. It's hard to explain."

"I get it, Harley. It was a massive change for you, but it sure looks like you have adjusted well, and from what I saw of your grandmother, you have someone in your life that cares very deeply for you. Consider yourself fortunate in that respect."

"Well, I definitely don't take it for granted. That's for sure."

"Good," Chris stated. "All right, enough with the heavy. Let's talk about our plans for the next few days."

The mood in the car changed dramatically. Abby leaned forward and asked, "So where should we go first?"

"Let's go to the campground, get ourselves settled in for the duration, and then rehash what we have learned. Going back over our findings may actually lead us to our next step. How does that sound?"

Harley and Anna felt that was as good a plan as any, so they nodded their assent, and the threesome continued on their way down the highway, discussing school activities and Chris's police career. Harley leaned back in his seat. It was good to be together again.

Arriving at the Triple C, they checked in, drove over to the cabin, and unloaded their luggage. They climbed the steps and walked across the small porch of the log cabin that would be their home for the next few days.

When they opened the doors, they found a set of bunk beds on one side of the cabin and a full size bed on the other side. The beds contained simple mattresses and no linens, which Harley, being experienced at this kind of camping, had realized.

Having anticipated this, he had told the other two to pack a sleeping bag or bring a set of sheets, depending on their preference. Harley rather enjoyed a sleeping bag, so he set his bags down, pulled out his sleeping bag, and turned to Abby. "Top or bottom?" he motioned at the bunks.

Chris cut in, "She can have the other bed, Harley. I can take one of the bunks."

Abby protested. "No, Chris, you have been nice enough to come along with us so we have supervision. It's the least we can do. Harley and I discussed this when we were in Michigan, and we both agreed that you should have it."

Harley nodded, and Chris shrugged, "If you're both sure, then fine by me."

Harley turned back to Abby, "Well?"

"Top," she answered promptly. "Always liked climbing up the ladder."

"Works for me," Harley responded, and promptly tossed his sleeping bag on the lower bunk, followed quickly by his luggage. "I'll take care of that later. You two want to get something to eat before we go off on our little adventure? I'm kind of hungry."

Chris and Abby looked at each other, nodded, and followed

Harley's lead by tossing their belongings on their respective beds. "I'm kind of hungry too, Chris," Abby put in. "Do you mind if we grab a bite now?"

"Looks like we all are on the same page. I could use something in my gut as well. Nice to see we are thinking alike already. Let's hope that is a good omen."

The trio quickly exited the cabin, locked the door behind them, and headed back to the rental car. Chris deftly maneuvered the car through the campground, out to the highway, and headed in the direction of Plymouth. "Fast food or café?" he asked.

"Café," the two teenagers choroused.

"Café it is," Chris laughed. Moments later he spotted a small restaurant ahead and pointed. "Okay?"

"Looks good to me," Harley said.

Chris pulled in the parking lot, entered a parking spot, and turned the engine off. "Let's eat."

Over a luncheon special of beef tips over noodles, which all three ordered, they began to discuss plans.

"So where should we begin?" Abby asked, as she placed a forkful of noodles and meat into her mouth.

"We're only a couple of miles from Plymouth, and I've done a little background research on this area," Chris began. "We could check out the replica *Mayflower*, and then maybe drive over to Plimoth Plantation. It's only a couple of miles from there."

Harley concurred, "That sounds good. I'm looking forward to seeing that, especially since we do have some info that may be helpful."

"The ship or the settlement?" Abby asked.

"Both, but the settlement will probably give us more clues than the ship."

"Why do you think that?"

"Because Stephen Hopkins' home is at Plimoth Plantation, and that is the connection I made between Plymouth and Jamestown."

Chris interrupted quietly, "Maybe we ought to rehash what we know somewhere a little more private."

Harley instantly understood why Chris had spoken in that manner. He nodded and continued in almost a whisper, "You're right, maybe in the car on the way over to the *Mayflower*?"

"Good idea," Chris commented.

The three finished their meal quietly, paid the bill, and strolled out into the summer sunshine. Harley breathed in the fresh air deeply. He was ready to do some investigating. He held the door open for Abby, clambered in beside her, and called across to Chris, "Okay, Hook, lead on."

Chris laughed, "As you wish, my lord." He pulled the car back onto the highway and headed for the city of Plymouth.

"Okay, Harley," Abby started, "let's go back over your hypothesis."

Harley responded by reaching into his pocket and pulling out a copy of the notes his father had made. He glanced at them a moment, recollecting all that had occurred previously to bring them all to this point. Finally he took a deep breath and began.

"Okay, let's start with the first entry. Bartholomew Gosnold was one of the captains of the three ships that came over to Jamestown. He did not like the location Newport had chosen at all, mostly due to the fact the area was mosquito infested,"

Abby added, "Quite ironic that he dies of malaria after only being there a couple of months, isn't it?"

"Ironic, maybe, but like my dad said, too many coincidences."

"What does that mean?" Abby asked.

"It means that maybe some other forces were at work there."

"Such as?" Chris asked.

"Not really sure, but what I do know is that Gosnold also explored here in 1602, at least the Cape Cod area, and now here we are. Coincidence? I don't think so. He must have known something about this place as well as what was going on at Jamestown. Plus, don't you find it more than coincidental that I found the letter, amulet, and his skull all lying together after the first tornado?"

"Agreed," Chris replied. "Continue."

"Okay, so then we know John Smith wrote this letter to Captain Newport." He pulled out a copy of the letter and looked at it for what seemed the thousandth time.

To Captain Newport, Kinde Sir,

Certain Gentlemen have, I fear, assalted Captaine Smith, thus leauing him sicke and weake thereof. As yet they are vnaware of our secret, one which must remaineth. Fearing discouerie, I hath diuided the remaining talismens, leauing one here with this discourse, and shall set saile for England. Time thvs passing awa y, Captain Gosnold shall protect said secret until which time, Kinde Sir, he shall reueal it to thyself.

Once such reuelation hath occurred, shovld I not recouer, wouldst pray thee reuege my death and vse talisman as seeth fit. From hence, I shall await yovr safe and quick returne, that wee may continve our endeauor. Hauing thvs by God's assistance being prouided with said information, bouldly proceed according to thy beste intentions.

Captaine John Smith

"From this we can determine that Smith and Newport both knew of the amulets and their connections to Atlantis, right?" Harley asked.

Abby responded, "Right, and we know that Smith was burned in an explosion, returned to England, and missed Newport in the process. That was when Newport and the *Sea Venture* shipwrecked in Bermuda, and they were stranded there until they built two smaller ships and made it to Jamestown the following year."

"Right," Harley replied. "Then there is the Stephen Hopkins

connection."

Chris interrupted, "Explain that one again, Harley."

Harley nodded. "Stephen Hopkins was on the *Sea Venture* with Newport, and he made it to Jamestown as well. Let's stop and think about their time together in Bermuda."

Abby commented, "You think that Newport said something to Hopkins, don't you?"

"Well, I find it more than coincidental that Hopkins and Smith had very similar encounters with the powers that be."

"What do you mean?" Chris asked.

"We know that Smith was despised in Jamestown and actually sentenced to death before Newport saved him. In the same way, Hopkins voiced displeasure on Bermuda with the governor and was going to be executed until others begged mercy for him, and the order was rescinded. Now I don't know if Newport was on his side or not, but I wouldn't doubt it."

"So what you're saying is that all this may have been a ploy on Newport's part to make things appear differently than they really were," Chris commented.

"I think so. I think that Newport confided in Hopkins, in case something went wrong on the trip from Bermuda to Jamestown. Of course neither was able to get the letter that Smith buried with Gosnold's body, and although both of them returned to England eventually, by the time Newport once again sailed to Jamestown, Gosnold's grave was lost. It wasn't found until after 1994 when the James Fort was discovered."

"What about Newport?" Anna asked. "If he came back on another resupply, why isn't he involved later on here at Plymouth?"

"I can answer that one," Chris intervened. "He joined the East India Company in 1613 and sailed to India. It says so in the notes. He came back to England in 1614."

"Right," Harley agreed, "and in the meantime, John Smith sailed to Plymouth, or at least Cape Cod, and reconnoitered the area. So now, by 1614, both Gosnold and Smith had been here, and we know that Stephen Hopkins comes here in 1620 on the *Mayflower*."

Chris again volunteered some information. "In the meantime, Newport had made a second trip to India, and from this one he never returned. He died in 1617 in India, never being able to finish off the investigation with Smith."

Abby was quietly looking over Harley's dad's notes. "How does John Rolfe fit into this?"

Harley answered that question. "You can see that Rolfe came to Jamestown as well, and that he was also on the *Sea Venture*. I have to believe that he was in on this as well because he returned to England with Pocahontas and met with Smith. I think that they, and Pocahontas, were discussing the second amulet that Smith left behind for Newport. Of course, Pocahontas never makes it back to America, but Rolfe does, and I have to believe he was searching for the location of Gosnold's grave, but he never found it."

"He died in 1622, so just a short time after the Pilgrims landed here in Plymouth, three of the major players in this game, Newport, Rolfe, and Pocahontas are dead," Harley concluded.

"So is Powhatan," Abby added.

"Right," Harley agreed, "leaving us with John Smith and Stephen Hopkins left to carry on their endeavor."

"Not just them, Harley," Chris again intervened.

"What do you mean? Who else?"

"Captain Christopher Jones, the owner and captain of the *Mayflower*."

"I was wondering about him being on the list. What makes you think he is part of this?"

Chris smiled, "Well since my namesake was involved in all of this, I dug into his past, and guess what I found?"

"What?" the other two chorused.

"Only this. Captain Christopher Newport, aka Captain Hook, and Captain Christopher Jones, are both from the same hometown-Harwich, England. See the connection?"

"Whoooa!" Harley breathed. "That means Jones may have been involved as well."

"Sure seems that way," Chris concluded, "but let's throw another piece into the puzzle."

Abby shook her head. "What else could you have found?"

"Do you see John Alden's name on that list? Know who he is?"

Harley said, "Well, yeah, he was on the *Mayflower*, and he is the one who was involved with Priscilla Mullins and Myles Standish. Kind of a love triangle, if I remember."

Abby added, "That's the Henry Wadsworth Longfellow story called *The Courtship of Myles Standish*."

"Oh," Harley continued, "my parents had some old books written by Longfellow. They are kind of family heirlooms, along with a bunch of other famous authors like Twain, Dickens, and Stevenson."

Abby giggled, "I remember watching *A Charlie Brown Thanksgiving*, and Linus talking about John Alden and Priscilla Mullins."

Harley laughed and replied, "I prefer *It's the Great Pumpkin, Charlie Brown*."

Chris shook his head, "Okay, okay, you two are getting way off the topic. So, yes, you have the right people, but here is a little known fact. John Alden and Captain Jones were related."

"What?" Harley and Abby gasped.

"They were cousins. Coincidence? I think not."

"Wow! Nice job finding all that out, Chris," Harley praised.

"No kidding!" Abby added on.

Chris laughed modestly. "All in a day's work. After all, I do need to hold up my end of this little adventure. Can't have you two doing all the work and making all the discoveries."

"Still, that's very cool. Amazing what we've been able to find,"

Harley rejoined.

Abby squeezed his hand. "I love it when you say 'we'."

He squeezed back. "None of us would ever be able to do this alone. We make a great team."

Chris nodded, "You're right, and we'll continue this conversation later."

"Why's that?" Harley asked.

"Because we're here. Look." Chris pointed out the window. "There she is, the *Mayflower II*.

Sure enough, they had arrived in downtown Plymouth, and there, gently bobbing in the tiny waves was a wooden vessel with sails furled and its size dwarfing the canoes, kayaks, and skiffs drawn up alongside it.

"Shall we take a tour?" Chris asked.

"Absolutely!" Abby cried. "Oh, this is going to be so much fun!"

Harley grinned at her. She was so passionate, and Harley loved watching how her eyes sparkled like the water on the bay. Between that and her smile, Harley was incapable of thinking clearly if he became too absorbed in staring at her.

Abby caught him staring, and purposely gave him a devilish grin that all but incapacitated him. He shook his head and tried to clear his thoughts. "What's the matter?" she smirked.

"You're still beautiful."

"You're still cute." With that she gave him a quick kiss directly on the lips, and then shoved him toward the door. "Now, come on, I want to go on the boat."

"Yes, boss," Harley grinned.

"And don't forget it either," Abby retorted.

———— ◖◉◗ ————

Harley, Abby, and Chris ambled over to where the replica ship was floating. First, however, they stopped at a large monument that overlooked the bay. Harley noted the circular pillars, which reminded him of a smaller version of the White House. Unlike the President's home, this monument was not a building, but rather an enclosure that stood above and protected the actual Plymouth Rock.

The trio walked over to the site, peered over an iron restraining fence, and noted the granite stone with 1620 inscribed on it. Harley also noted that the rock appeared to have cracked in half, and that it must have been repaired.

Chris pointed that out. "Apparently in the 1700s people in this area tried to move it, and it split in half. They repaired it not all that long ago. I think I heard that they also put some protective sealer or something on it to stop erosion. Apparently it used to be huge compared to now. Plus, before it was set up like this, people would go down on the beach and break off pieces of it as souvenirs."

Abby commented sadly, "That's too bad. People just don't think before they act. I was always taught to leave only footprints and take only pictures. In that way, future generations would be able to see the same things I was seeing."

"That's a terrific motto to live by, Abby. You were taught well." Chris replied.

"Thanks, Chris," she said quietly, and Harley knew that the two were both recalling the incident with Abby's parents the previous year. Despite what had occurred, Harley had found out much about them over the past year. They had been hard-working, patriotic people, but they unfortunately had chosen a path that ultimately led to their destruction. That second tornado at Jamestown may have saved Harley's life, but it had cost both Abby and him dearly.

"Time to change the subject," he thought to himself. Aloud, he said, "Photo shoot? We might as well make some memories while we are here."

The other two whole-heartedly agreed, and soon they were

taking turns posing by the enclosure or leaning over the barrier to take selfies with the famous rock lying on the beach below.

Tiring of that, they proceeded over to the replica ship, the *Mayflower II*. There, they needed to make a decision. "Should we just get a combo ticket for the ship and the settlement?" Abby asked.

"Makes sense to do that," Chris concluded, "since we will be going there eventually."

With that decision made they continued to the ship, paid the admission fees, and walked inside the exhibit area. They spent the next hour checking out photographs of the replica ship as it was built in 1957, navigation techniques that were used in that time period, and most notably the passenger list, which they all crowded around to verify some of the names.

Among the passenger and crew list were some from Harley's dad's list-Stephen Hopkins, John Alden, Captain Jones- along with some of the other very familiar Pilgrim names-Myles Standish, Priscilla Mullins, William Bradford, and William Brewster, just to name a few.

All three of them were thinking the same thing. Somehow, members of this ship had known about Atlantis. How many was uncertain, but the connections between Roanoke, Jamestown, and Plymouth were so strong, that there could be no doubt that it was more than just coincidence.

Finally, Chris pulled away long enough to break the trance that seemed to hold them to that spot in the exhibit area. "Are we ready to check out the ship?"

"Oh, yes, let's go," Abby said. "I'm looking forward to seeing what it was like to be on that ship."

As they boarded the *Mayflower II*, Harley realized that the ship was not as large as it had seemed from the Plymouth Rock enclosure. As a matter of fact, it was very small. Listening to some of the re-enactors, he found the ship to be barely over 100 feet long and about

25 feet wide.

"Just think, Abby," he whispered, "they sailed all the way across the Atlantic Ocean on this. I'm not sure I'd feel all that safe on the Great Lakes, let alone going 3000 miles on it in the open ocean."

"Sure is beautiful though, isn't it?" she murmured, leaning on the rail and staring out at the water

"Not as beautiful as you though," Harley squeezed her from behind.

"Looks like I've done a good job training you, anyway," she smiled, and squeezed his arm.

They continued the tour, and as they toured they learned that this replica ship was almost identical to the original. A couple of differences were the staircase that led below deck would have just been a ladder during the 1600s, and of course, there were some electrical lights that dimly lit the below deck areas. Other than that and a few other minor details, the ship was identical.

Harley shook his head. "Just imagine stuffing 100 people into this little ship for all those weeks. Unbelievable!"

Chris grinned at him. "Don't like close quarters, Harley?"

"Well, depends on whom I'm in close quarters with," he nodded at Abby.

Chris laughed and turned to Abby. "You're right. You trained him well."

Abby slid her arm around Harley's waist. "Well worth the effort, though," she grinned slyly at Chris.

Harley could feel himself turning red. Sometimes he wondered if paying Abby compliments was too much. He wasn't doing it for any particular reason, other than speaking his thoughts. Still, she didn't seem to mind or find it overdone, so he concluded he should just continue to be himself and say what he felt. After all, hadn't his mother always told him that honesty was the best policy?

Of course, that sent him to thinking of the Atlantis information he had kept a secret during his time at Roanoke and Jamestown. If he had turned all that info over to the authorities immediately, was it possible that some of the deaths could have been prevented?

Now, he had more information that his dad had found, and again he had kept it between just the other two and himself. Could he be setting himself up for another disaster? He shook his head, attempting to rid his mind of those thoughts.

Abby noted the motion, but mistook it for embarrassment. "Am I bothering you?" she smiled sweetly.

"Never," Harley declared. "Never, ever."

"Good, now let's go back up on deck and take a few more pictures. I want this to be a memorable trip too."

They took some time to photograph themselves, and then they came to a consensus that photos of the surrounding area might not be a bad idea either, just in case they came across a clue and weren't in Plymouth at the time.

They walked back toward the car, passing the Plymouth Rock enclosure, and stopping to take a photo of the sign by the park area. The sign read:

PLYMOUTH ROCK
LANDING PLACE OF THE
PILGRIMS
1620
COMMONWEALTH OF MASSACHUSETTS

Chris suggested, "Let's take a walk through the park and get some photos of the beach area. Then we can walk up and down the street here and check out the shops."

The other two agreed, and they spent the next hour wandering around the bay area. Finally, they all had seen enough, so they mutually agreed that it was time to head back to the campground, with a quick stop at a grocery store to pick up some food and cooking supplies.

Since all of them had flown in, none had brought any real camping equipment, so they grabbed some cheap pans, pots and a Styrofoam cooler, along with food and beverage choices.

Harley reminded them, "We can get ice, and anything else we might forget, at the campground. They have a store there, and anyway we will need firewood for the campfire."

"Seems like you have this camping thing down pat. Can you cook too?" Chris queried.

"Some," Harley said. "Thankfully I rode with Dad for two summers, so I really learned a lot from him. He was always so proactive that I decided to make it one of my goals to do some preplanning and not allow too many things to surprise me and put me in reaction mode."

"Looks like your dad did a fine job. I'm sorry I didn't get to know him better, but at least I was able to meet him those couple of times. He was a good man, Harley, and you can be very proud to be his son."

"Thanks, Chris, I appreciate it." He turned to Abby. "Think you have all you want or need?"

She smiled her devilish little grin, walked up to him, and placed a smooch right on his kisser, right in front of the checkout worker. "Now I do."

Harley turned red, Abby and the cashier laughed, and Chris grinned at Harley's predicament.

"C'mon, big boy, let's go. Looks like you got a little sun today."

"What do you mean?"

"Your skin is just a bit pink right now, if you know what I mean."

"You, too? That's not fair ganging up on me. Be nice to me. I'm paying for this, you know." With that he pulled out his wallet and handed the still grinning cashier the money for their groceries and assorted sundries.

"Good luck with those two," the cashier smiled at him as she handed back his change.

"No kidding, huh? With friends like that, who needs enemies?"

"Awww!" Abby ruffled his hair. "My big, bad boyfriend feeling a bit victimized?"

That sent the others laughing again, and finally Abby relented long enough to grab one of the bags, hand it to Chris, stuff two more bags into Harley's arms, and grabbed the last one herself.

Once they reached the car and set their supplies in the trunk, Harley grabbed Abby and spun her back toward him, taking her completely by surprise. Before she had time to react, he bent down and kissed her quickly, pulled away, and said haughtily, "There! Now I got what I needed too."

For possibly the first time in her life, Abby appeared speechless. Still, she wasn't about to let him win that easily. Once she composed herself, she threw him that one killer smile he could not resist, and responded, "Well, that's more like it."

With that, she spun back to the car, hopped in, and pulled the door shut before Harley had a chance to move. Then she locked the door.

Chris, who had witnessed the entire encounter, stated matter-of-factly, "You might be walking home."

Harley took his cue, knocked on the window, and said sweetly, "Oh, Abby, may I please be allowed into the car?"

She called through the closed window, "Just so long as you know who's in charge."

"Yes, boss."

"Hope you don't ever *really* make her mad," Chris quipped.

"No kidding, eh?" Harley replied, as Abby hit the unlock button and he pulled open the door and sat down beside the young woman who seemed to have complete and utter control of him.

The adventurers drove back to the campground, stopped at the lodge to grab some firewood, and then headed over to their site to prepare a dinner over a campfire. It was going to be an easy night for them, just hot dogs, chips, and veggies. This gave them some time to unwind, and since it was still not all that late, a decision was made to hit the swimming pool and/or the hot tub before settling in for a night around a campfire under the stars.

After their supper and swim, Harley got the fire going again, and they all sat down on some stumps that were conveniently located near the fire pit. For once the conversation was steered away from Atlantis. Harley was curious about Chris, so he asked, "Chris, Abby and I have spent a lot of time together since we first met, so we've gotten to know each other pretty well, but we were kind of hoping you would tell us about what it was like growing up in Virginia. Would you mind sharing?"

Chris looked pleased actually, as if he hadn't had too many people ask about his life. "Well sure, what would you like to know?"

Abby jumped into the conversation. "Anything really, like your childhood, or joining the police force, or if you have a significant other. We would just like to hear some stories, if you don't mind."

"Well, okay. I think I told you I had some family in Newport News when you were at my place. I was actually born and raised there. My parents are still there now, along with my one sister. She's married now, has one child, and another on the way."

"So you're an uncle?" Harley cut in.

"Yep. My nephew is three." He stopped for a moment, and then laughed. "He thinks it's cool that his uncle has a hook. He makes me watch *Peter Pan* with him. Guess that makes me Uncle Captain Hook."

The two teenagers smiled at his joke, but knowing what had occurred, what placed Chris in this situation, prevented normal jocularity. Chris didn't seem to notice, and he continued with his explanation.

"Let's see, what else? Oh, becoming a police officer. I went to the academy straight out of high school. I always wanted to be a cop. I also thought about being part of the K-9 unit. Since I'm single, it would be nice to have some company."

"No female friend then?" Abby asked hesitantly.

"Nope, not right now. Had a girlfriend for a while in high school and while I was in the academy, but she broke it off with me."

"May I ask why?" Abby asked quietly.

"She was afraid of becoming a widow at a young age." Chris paused, as if to contemplate what he should say next. "She knows how dangerous it is to be a police officer. There is no guarantee about coming home when you leave in the morning. Anyway, she found love elsewhere. I think I heard he's into technology or something like that. Safer than police work anyway." Chris absent-mindedly tossed a stick in the fire.

"How old are you anyway, Chris?" Harley asked, trying to change what he realized must have been a touchy subject. "Mid-twenties I'm guessing."

"Not bad, Harley, I'm 29 actually. I'll be 30 in two weeks."

Abby immediately became excited. "Well, then, you have to let us take you out to a nice restaurant to celebrate, even if it has to be a little early."

Harley agreed. "Yeah, sounds like we are going to just miss being here for your birthday, so Abby is right. We are going to celebrate one night this week, and no arguing about it either. As a matter-of-fact, we'll make a day of it. Is there something you would like to do in the area, other than constantly search for Atlantis?"

Chris leaned back on his stump. "You guys don't need to do that."

Abby cut him off. "That's right! We don't need to. We *want* to."

"That's right, Chris," Harley added. "We really would like to treat you to something special. So, anything come to mind?"

Chris took a deep breath. "Well, we are already so close to Boston, so I figured we might go see the Revolutionary War sites one day this week anyway, and if you weren't interested I'd hang here an extra day or two and do it on my own..." His voice trailed off.

"No, that's a good idea too, and I think we should all go see Bunker Hill, Lexington and Concord, and even maybe hit Salem and Gloucester," Harley suggested, "but it sounds like you have something else in mind."

"Well, are you two sports fans at all?"

"Sure," they chorused.

"I'd really like to see the Basketball Hall of Fame over in Springfield. It's about two hours from here. What do you think?"

Harley liked the idea, seeing as he was on the varsity basketball team, along with the football and baseball teams. "I'd love to go there! What about you, Abby?"

"Absolutely! I play for our high school team, and it would be great to see the Hall."

"Well, there you go, Chris," Harley finished. "It looks like we are going to the Basketball Hall of Fame for your birthday!"

The teenagers seemed almost more excited than Chris at the prospect, but he was still all smiles. "So when do you want to go?" he asked.

"I say tomorrow," Abby stated. "That way we don't go overboard here at Plymouth, get so wrapped up in our search that we completely forget about it."

Harley liked the idea too. As much as he wanted to hit Plimoth Plantation and find out more about the Pilgrims, he was also desirous of doing something for Chris. After all, Chris had saved his life, and no amount of tours or gifts could pay him back for that. He had lost an arm as well, and noting Chris's physique, he figured that Chris had probably been a pretty good hoopster in his own right.

"Yes, let's go tomorrow, bright and early. Why don't we see what else is there, in case we have any extra time?"

"No need," Chris countered. "I already looked. It's the birthplace of Dr. Seuss, so there is some cool stuff to see. That is, if you're not too old to enjoy Dr. Seuss."

"You're never too old for Dr. Seuss," Abby responded.

"There's also the armory where many of the weapons for the American Revolution were made," Chris added. "Pretty cool pistol display, I heard."

"Sounds like a trip to Springfield is the plan for tomorrow then," Harley decided. "I'd say we should get an early start, so that we can have a whole day there. 6 a.m. too early to get going?"

"Fine by me," Chris answered, "but if we are going to start out that early maybe we should clean up tonight and make an early evening of it. It's almost dark now, so if we've decided, then I think I'll hit the showers."

Abby started to get up too. "I think I'll do the same. Otherwise my hair will take forever to dry in the morning."

Harley decided to wait by the fire while they were in the showers. He wanted to keep an eye on the flames, as well as have a few moments alone with his thoughts.

"He's all alone. I can tell he still really loves that girl. He chose his profession over love. Serving and protecting others. Wonder if he ever regrets doing that, especially after losing his arm?"

Harley sighed, stirred the dying embers, and then extinguished them with some dirt. Finally he grabbed his toiletry bag and headed for the showers. Tomorrow would be a long day. Hopefully it would be filled with fun and wonderful memories.

Dawn came early, and the trio rolled out of bed slowly, took a hike to the restroom to brush their teeth and freshen up, and then headed out toward Springfield.

"Were you a hoopster, Chris?" Harley asked, as they were heading down the highway.

"Yes, I played in high school. I had the opportunity to play in college actually."

"Wow!" Abby perked up. "That's pretty impressive. What schools were looking at you?"

"Well, some of the smaller schools in Virginia, like Division 3, but I did get an offer from William and Mary."

"Holy cow!" exclaimed Harley. "Why did you turn that down?"

"I wanted to be a cop. That was more important to me than a basketball scholarship." He stopped for a moment. "I suppose I could have waited to go to the academy. Meghan asked me to do that, but I said no." Chris paused again, as if questioning himself about the decision he had made.

"Meghan?" Abby asked.

"Yeah, the girl I was seeing in high school. She tried to support me in my decision, but as time went by, we drifted apart. I just don't think she was prepared to be married to a cop."

"Married?" Harley questioned.

"I guess I should have told you that I actually asked her to marry me when we graduated high school, but our engagement was eventually broken off because of the academy. It's just a little difficult to talk about."

"Sorry if we brought up a sore subject, Chris," Abby apologized.

"Oh, don't worry about that. I made a choice, and I have to live with it. We all make choices. Some work out as planned and some don't. If we don't take risks and go after our goals, there's no growth. You just stagnate."

Abby replied, "Well, still, Harley and I will try to cool it with the lovebird stuff. Right, Harley."

Harley readily agreed, but Chris nixed that immediately. "Are you kidding me? Do you know how refreshing it is to see two young people who care about each other so much? You two have something pretty special, whether you know it or not. Anyone who knows you at all can see it without even trying. You make a great pair, and I hope it lasts a long time. Now, no more feeling sorry for me. I am planning on having a great day in Springfield with my two new friends, and then spend the rest of the time solving the mystery of Atlantis. Understand?"

"Absolutely," Abby said.

"Agreed," Harley added.

"Good, now let's talk some hoops. Who are your favorite teams, college and pro? And how are your own teams looking for your senior years?"

That question altered the conversation immediately, and they spent the rest of the time in the car discussing the NBA, NCAA, and their high school teams, arguing what players were the best, which teams were likely to win championships, and what coaches should get fired. All in all, it was an entertaining drive.

Since the Hall did not open until 10:00, they decided to grab breakfast, since their arrival preceded the doors opening. A café not far from the Hall of Fame did the trick, and they continued their heated sports discussion.

It was overshadowed by their time at the Hall of Fame though. Touring the beautiful building situated by the Connecticut River, checking out the Hall of Famers, and revisiting the story of Dr. Naismith inventing the game made the morning pass quickly. Before they knew it, they were finding themselves at the end of the tour.

There was a unanimous vote to catch a late lunch, hit the Springfield Armory for an hour or two, and made a quick stop to see the bronze statues of some of the Dr. Seuss characters, before heading back toward Plymouth.

All in all, it was an exhilarating day, and Harley found himself very nearly exhausted as they drove along. Abby, too, seemed worn out. She leaned on his chest as Harley put his arm around her.

"You two going to stay awake for the ride back?" Chris grinned over at the two teenagers.

"We'll try, but no promises," laughed Harley. "We promise not to leave you hanging on the ride home. How about some music?"

"What do you like?"

"I like classic rock. Abby likes it too, as well as some country. What about you, Chris?"

"About the same as you two, with a little folk music thrown in for good measure. Let's see what's on."

They settled on one station, and the rest of the way home they sang along and be-bopped to many familiar songs, laughing at some of the antics put on display for each other, including air guitars, air drums, and butchering the words to some of the songs. All in all, it was a great time, and they arrived back in high spirits from a very successful day.

Harley lit the campfire, and they proceeded to make a dinner of burgers over the fire, followed by some s'mores and a couple of good old ghost stories. Chris was quite good at telling scary stories, and with Abby snuggled up against him for protection from the monsters, Harley was about as happy as he could be.

"This is the way every day should be," he thought to himself. "Fun with friends, a little travel, and a little adventure. What more could a person want?" He frowned for a moment. "Don't go there," he ordered himself. "Just enjoy the moment." For the rest of the evening, that is exactly what he did.

The following morning, after some breakfast by the fire and a quick shower, the three adventurers headed off to see Plimoth Plantation. At the entrance, Harley noted a large picture of a native Wampanoag on one side of what resembled a wooden covered bridge. On the other side was a picture of a Pilgrim. It was not a bridge, however, but a walkway that led to the Wampanoag settlement.

As they entered the plantation, the first sign they came across told them that they would be seeing a Wampanoag home that would have been similar to one where Chief Massasoit's councilmen would have resided. In fact, this particular councilman, Hobbamock, along with Squanto, was the key to the survival of the Pilgrims that first winter.

Massasoit also had instructed the other two to be diplomats and attempt to befriend the strangers. Habbomock was never as well-known as Squanto in American history, but he had apparently been loved by the English, possibly because he had converted to Christianity.

Harley, Abby, and Chris finally came alongside the actual dwelling, and upon entering discovered a woman sitting inside. She was working on some piece of clothing as she sat near a small fire that made the enclosure quite a bit smokier than Harley had imagined.

The fire itself was of interest. Rather than having a bunch of pieces of wood in a pile, there was a long branch that extended almost to the doorway, with just the first foot or so of it ablaze. The woman, a Wampanoag herself, informed them that all that was required to keep the fire going was to break off the burning piece and then slide the small log forward and add it to the top of the burning piece.

After speaking with her about her ancestry and some of her day to day activities, they exited the small hut and studied the Native American garden. Unlike gardens of today, where people tend to plant in rows, the gardens were simply mounds with beans, squash, and corn growing out of each mound. The Three Sisters, as they were known, were the staple for Natives and English alike in the early years of Plimoth's existence.

Also outside were two canoes that had been burned and chopped out. They were almost identical to the ones that Harley had seen at Jamestown. No one was around to tell them no, so they climbed in one and took some photographs.

Then the trio followed the trail through the woods and came upon a large, fenced in area that Harley realized must be Plimoth Plantation itself. From just outside, Harley noted that there were a few cows grazing on a small hillside.

Once inside the gate, they noticed many huts that were the houses of the original Pilgrims. A dirt road led across the plantation. It met up with a crossroad that extended down toward the bay, as well as up toward a huge two-story meetinghouse that was located at the top of the gradual rise from the bay. This location afforded the Pilgrims the best view of the bay in case of attack.

Abby began exploring inside some of the homes, and Chris and Harley followed her around. They were pleasantly surprised to see some very beautiful bed quilts and other housewares that the Pilgrims would have brought along on the *Mayflower*.

A second surprise was that each of the re-enactors actually spoke in Old English, so when they were conversing, it was as if Harley had been transported back to the 1620s. They spoke of the Spanish possibly invading and how their first winter had been so difficult. Each of the actors had actually studied a particular Pilgrim, and now was playing that role full time and lived and worked as the original group had, right down to using the tools and instruments of the day.

After entering a few of the replica homes, Chris suggested, "How about going up to the meetinghouse and getting a view of the entire plantation? Might help us envision some things."

"Good idea," Abby replied. Harley nodded his assent as well.

Upon entering the meetinghouse, they found themselves in the middle of what appeared to be a prayer service. It was being led by a costumed individual who was in the midst of the Lord's Prayer. The three stopped long enough to allow him to finish the prayer. Then they weaved their way behind and through some of the other tourists to the set of stairs that led to the second story.

They quietly climbed the steps, and when they reached the second level, they found themselves staring at a number of cannons, strategically placed at shuttered openings. Peering out one side of the building, they could see the entire plantation spread out below them, running almost all the way to the bay. It was an excellent observation point, both for the Pilgrims in their day, as well as for the three present day explorers.

Chris was the first to speak, "There's a website that shows the layout of Plimoth Plantation by name."

"What do you mean, 'by name'?" Abby asked.

"I mean that each house is labeled, so we can figure out who lived where. For example, according to the website, William Bradford's home was right at the corner of the two cross streets, and Stephen Hopkins' home was directly across the road from him."

Harley gazed down at the plantation. "So which side of the road is it?"

"Looking toward the bay," Chris explained, "Bradford's would be on the left side of the road, just this side of the crossroad. Hopkins' home would be on the same side of the road as Bradford, but across the intersection, closer to the bay."

"We haven't been in those two yet, have we?" Abby asked.

"No," Harley answered, "we looked through the ones on the other side of the street."

"Well, then, I'm assuming we are going to head to Hopkins' house next," Abby concluded.

"Seems like the next logical step," Chris put in. "Want some photos from here before we head back down?"

"Yes," Abby responded, dragging Harley over to one of the cannons and posing as if she was about to fire one of them.

"Who do you think you are?" Chris laughed. "Molly Pitcher Hays?"

"Wrong time period, Chris," retorted Abby, "she was in the American Revolution."

"Impressive," he replied.

"I pay attention in history class, at least a lot more than I used to," she chuckled.

"Well, that's good. Never know when we are going to need a piece of information that we have learned."

Harley was listening to their banter, but at the same time he was attempting to recall a piece of information he had read about Plimoth Plantation, but he couldn't recall it at that moment. Finally, after the photo op was finished, he said, "Let's head down to Hopkins' home. Maybe there will be something inside that will give us some sort of clue."

The others agreed, followed him down the steps, again wound their way through the tourists, and then headed down the hill in the direction of the Stephen Hopkins' home.

Stepping inside was again like stepping back 400 years into the past. All of the décor was as it would have appeared in the early 17th century. Perusing the area in silence, peering at every piece in the home as closely as possible, nothing jumped out at them.

"Of course," Chris broke the quiet, "this is just a replica of his real home. Obviously the original homes of all these people have been destroyed, rebuilt, or built over."

That statement finally broke through the mental block that Harley was having. "Of course," he echoed. "This isn't Plimoth Plantation. The whole thing is a re-creation. The real Plimoth Plantation was built right down by the *Mayflower*! We're searching in the wrong spot!"

Both Chris and Abby both looked surprised, and a bit abashed, that they had not realized this indisputable truth.

"You're right, Harley," Chris agreed. "We have been so excited about searching for the hidden that we overlooked the obvious. I think I read that somewhere too. Still, we are here right now, and we may yet learn something of value from one of these re-enactors. After all, they have studied the real Pilgrims in depth, so they know more than we do about the actual lives and times of Hopkins and the others."

Abby agreed, "That's true. Why don't we spend some time finding out who the actors are portraying, and ask them some questions? We might get lucky."

The trio decided to stay together during this process, taking into consideration that if they split up, one of them may miss something, where the others may come to some important conclusion. "Three heads are better than one," Harley resolved.

It took a couple of hours to interview as many of the actors as they could find, but try as they might, there was no enlightening answer forthcoming.

Disappointed, but not beaten, they decided to continue to the third part of the plantation, which was the craft center. There they found a variety of objects being created, some by Native Americans, such as real arrows that could be used with a bow. Others were creating clay pots and assorted earthenware plates, cups, and saucers. The lady working the wheel was extremely talented, speaking and working on various pieces without missing a beat. Just as in Williamsburg the previous year, Harley was amazed at the talent.

"I remember trying to do that in art class. My vase kept flopping over," he stated ruefully.

The lady laughed, "You know what they say, 'Practice, practice, practice.'"

Harley grinned, "Definitely not the first time I heard that."

Chris had been observing the woodworking area. Not a power

tool was in sight. "Look at that chair!" he whispered in awe to Abby and Harley, who had joined him across the room.

In front of them was what appeared to be a throne-like chair, with immaculate scrollwork, and contrasting red and black colors recessed within the scrollwork. It was incredible!

"Wonder what something like that would go for?" Harley murmured.

"You can take it home with you for $7000," stated one of the workers who had overheard the comment.

"Petty cash," Abby rejoined. "Maybe we'll take two."

The others laughed at that, and all three praised the workers on their abilities and talents. One of the craftsmen mentioned that some of the objects could be found in the gift shop at the Visitor's Center, so the trio made it a point upon leaving the craft area to head directly to that building.

"I want to get some sort of souvenir from here," Abby stated, "maybe a piece of pottery or some Native American jewelry. What about you two?"

Chris commented first. "Something by one of the woodworkers, I imagine. They are really talented."

Harley added, "I'll just take the chair. Think it will fit in my carry-on bag?"

The other two grinned at Harley's humor. He continued, "I'm like you, Chris, something made of wood. That was just way too impressive."

They spent almost an hour in the Henry Hornblower II Visitor Center, as it was named. Finally, each was able to choose something that they could have as a keepsake. Harley took note that Chris also had purchased a small Native American made bracelet. He stared at it quizzically. Chris caught his glance and smiled sheepishly.

"Christmas present," he explained. "Probably shouldn't, but I'll send it to Meghan...just because."

Harley nodded, not trusting his voice to say anything. Chris must have felt about Meghan the way that Harley felt about Abby. It was more than disappointing that his new friend had not found that special someone to share his life. Then Harley realized that Chris actually had. It just wasn't meant to be.

Abby had just finished paying for her souvenirs and walked up to the two young men. She sensed something was amiss. "Everything okay?" She glanced back and forth between the two.

Harley recovered first, "Yeah, we were just trying to figure out what we should do next."

"Well, I say let's eat before we do anything. I'm starving," Abby commanded.

The other two were all in agreement to that proposal, and as they made their way to the car, Abby pulled ahead. Chris whispered, "Thanks, Harley. Sometimes it's just hard. I wish I could let go, but when you find the one, you just know it." Harley nodded.

"C'mon, slowpokes, you walk like a couple of grandmas. I take that back. Grandma Larson and Grandma Schultz could outdo you two any day," she taunted haughtily.

That broke the subdued conversation. Harley sprinted toward Abby, who let out a delighted scream as he twirled her around and around.

"You're making me dizzy," she complained good-naturedly, when he finally stopped and set her back on the ground.

"Last thing I would ever call you is dizzy," Harley countered, knowing that Abby would have some sort of comeback. He wasn't disappointed.

"Call me dizzy, and you'll be calling an ambulance next. Got it?" Abby brandished her fist at him.

"Yes, boss."

"Just keep remembering that."

Chris interrupted the war of words. "Well, boss," directing his comments at Abby, "where and what would you like to eat?"

"How about we go back into Plymouth and find a seafood place. I could go for some clam chowder. Like they say, 'When in Rome…'"

"Or in this case, New England," Chris quipped dryly, "but some clam chowder does sound good. Maybe there is some place serving a buffet, so we can try a bunch of different foods."

Harley and Abby like that idea, so they traveled back downtown near the *Mayflower II*, parked the car, and started walking up and down the street until they came to a restaurant that advertised a buffet. They turned in there, and for the next hour or so enjoyed the samplings that were offered.

"Anyone leaves here hungry, it's their own fault," Chris declared, heading back up to the buffet for his third plateful.

"You said it," Harley agreed, as he too headed back to the buffet. "The chowder and shrimp have been great, but it's time to load up on crab."

"You better not be a crab if you eat too much," Abby warned. "Eyes bigger than your stomach, you know."

"Yeah, yeah, yeah," Harley replied, "but I don't see you stopping any time soon either."

"Well," Abby sighed, "guess I'll just have all my clothes taken out a couple of inches." She got up and headed for the food line as well.

They finished their meal in high spirits, and after the bill was paid, they walked back outside onto the sidewalk of Main Street, and then turned down North Street to stroll back toward water, as well as the rental car. Reaching Pilgrim Memorial State Park, they strolled around, just enjoying the scenery and struggling to work off the large meal they had just devoured.

"Still plenty of daylight. Any suggestions?" Harley asked.

Chris was the first to reply. "Let's take a look at exactly where Hopkins' real home was. They all took out their phones and began searching for any information that would be helpful. Abby found it first. "It says here that the crossroad at Plimoth Plantation is now at Main Street and Leyden. Looks like that is over two blocks from where we came down. Shall we head over there?"

Chris responded by saying, "After that, let's continue beyond there a little farther."

"What's farther up?" Harley asked.

"Burial Hill, where a number of the first Pilgrims were buried. Considering all that occurred at Jamestown, I would say a visit to a cemetery might be useful."

"How'd you find that?" Abby asked.

"Different website. Also says that they may be doing some archaeological digs there. Coincidence?"

"Nope," Harley rejoined. "Connection. Let's go."

They walked over to Leyden Street and proceeded back up the incline until they reached the corner at Main Street.

"Okay, so this building right here would be where Stephen Hopkins' home would have been, and across Main Street is where William Bradford's home would have been," Chris explained.

"You don't suppose they'd let us go digging in their basement, do you?" Abby quipped.

"Doubtful," Chris replied. "As a police officer, I would advise against breaking and entering as well."

"So now what?" Harley asked, looking around.

Chris pointed farther up Leyden Street. "Let's go check out what's going on up there at the cemetery."

They crossed Main Street, continued up to School Street, and then looked across at a large cemetery. Chris was already punching something into his phone.

"Hey, this place could help. There's a whole list of famous people buried here, including Governor Bradford, William Brewster, and Squanto, just to name a few. It also looks like they are doing a dig here, trying to find the original palisades of the plantation. From what I see here, they have to be careful not to disturb the graves." He pocketed his phone. "Want to go explore the cemetery?"

"Yes," Abby and Harley chorused, excited at the opportunity to find any kind of clue.

They spent the remainder of the daylight examining graves, especially noting the most famous grave-William Bradford. Unfortunately, Stephen Hopkins' grave was nowhere to be found. "Where did you say Stephen Hopkins was buried, Harley?" Chris asked.

Harley replied, "No one knows. Hard to believe that. He was an important person in the colony, especially during the first years. All of his interactions with Squanto and Massasoit are well documented. All anyone knows for sure is that he asked to be buried near his wife."

"Where was the last place he lived?" asked Abby.

"Here. He died in 1644. What I find interesting is that when he wrote his will, William Bradford and Myles Standish were his witnesses. Who better to trust with information about Atlantis than the governor and the military leader of the colony? I have to believe that since Hopkins was getting himself into a lot of trouble in the colony later on, maybe this information was getting to him."

"What do you mean, getting into trouble?" Abby asked.

"He opened a tavern, started selling alcohol, was fined many times for allowing men to become drunk in his establishment, and even fined once for committing battery on another man from the colony. It looks like he was having a difficult time at the end, especially with his wife dying a couple of years earlier. Maybe the folks of Plymouth just buried him in an unmarked grave because of the trouble he had caused."

"Soooo, he could actually be buried right here somewhere?" Chris concluded.

"I would say that it is a real possibility," Harley agreed. "The other cemetery that holds significant Pilgrims is about 10 miles from here. That's the Myles Standish Burial Ground. Standish is obviously the most famous person buried there. Just another bit of interesting trivia, John and Priscilla Alden are buried there too."

"Wow! Even in death those three are still connected. That's really cool…or really creepy," Abby shivered.

Harley smiled grimly. "Well, at least we have a number of pieces to this puzzle to examine. I'm thinking we should probably do a little library work. My dad and mom kept finding clues in the writings, not to mention the two pieces found at Roanoke and Jamestown. Maybe we should head back to the campground for the evening, do a little internet research, and see if anyone else wrote anything that might raise a red flag."

Chris looked at Harley with admiration. "That's a great idea, Harley. While reading isn't my strongest suit, maybe we can make a list of people that have written journals and/or letters that have been electronically reproduced. Then we can split them up and look for any clues."

"Well, not my idea of fun either," Abby commented, "but sitting around a fire and relaxing after a long day of touring sounds pretty good to me."

"Okay, then," Harley finished, "let's head back, get some dinner, and see if we can make any more connections."

Down the hill they headed, together, yet each lost in their own thoughts.

—————— ((()) ——————

After heading back to the campground, fixing a dinner over the fire, and cleaning up both the cabin and themselves, the three began their investigation into writings from various early colonists. While Chris and Abby began by looking at some of the Pilgrims, Harley decided he wanted to see what else John Smith had written.

Proceedings of the English Colony of Virginia was the first writing that Harley perused. Harley found out that John Smith had published it in 1612, four years after *True Relation*, the book that had given his father and him clues during their time at Jamestown and Williamsburg.

Harley found two more works by Smith entitled *Generall Historie of Virginia* (1624), and *The True Adventures and Observations of Captain John Smith* (1630). He recalled a conversation with his dad that Smith had never mentioned the Pocahontas incident until the 1624 book was published. Because of that oddity, Harley decided to concentrate more on that particular text.

Finding nothing that jumped out at him, Harley noticed that Smith had written *A Description of New England* in 1616. Since he was literally sitting in New England as he researched, he decided to inspect that particular piece of prose also.

Suddenly, something in the text jumped out at him. "Hey, you guys! I think I found something!"

"What?" Chris and Abby chorused.

"Take a look at this and tell me what you notice."

"Where exactly do you want us to look?" Abby asked.

"Page 4. Don't just look at the words. Look at it as a whole."

> *liue or die the slaue of scorne & infamy, if (hauing*
> *meanes) I make it not apparent; please God to*
> *blesse me but from such accidents as are beyond my*
> *power and reason to preuent. For my labours, I desire*
> *but such conditions as were promised me out*
> *of the gaines; and that your Highnesse*
> *would daigne to grace this Work, by*
> *your Princely and fauourable*
> *respect vnto it, and*
> *know mee*
> *to be*
>
> *Your Highnesse true*
> *and faithfull seruant,*
> *Iohn Smith.*

"What do you think?" Harley asked.

Neither of the others responded right away. Harley realized that he had begun to think like his father, as well as seeing things that could be open to conjecture, so he decided it was necessary to prod the others along.

"What do you notice about the shape of the writing?"

Chris answered first, "Looks like a V, I guess."

Abby added, "Kind of looks like someone centered it on the page." She looked at Harley. By the look on his face, she could tell that he had hoped she and Chris had seen something else.

"Okay, so you don't see anything special. How about what is actually written?"

Chris and Abby again stared at the words, rereading the text and thinking about what it said.

Chris asked, "What is this exactly, Harley? Obviously there is something here that has you so animated. Tell us what you're thinking."

Harley took a deep breath. "Okay, first of all, this is an account from John Smith called *A Description of New England*. He wrote this in 1616, after he had come to New England, been captured by French pirates, escaped, and made his way back to England."

"What made you think to look at that?" Abby asked.

"Well, since he was involved in Jamestown, I thought that maybe he might still have something to do with Atlantis later on. He was the kind of guy who liked to have his hand in all kinds of explorations. I can't believe he would have given up just because he was injured in that gunpowder explosion and returned to England."

"Okay," Chris cut in, "but what is it you think you found?"

"Right. Sorry I got off topic. This part of the book is called an epistle dedicatory. This particular piece is written to Prince Charles of England."

"Wow! That's going right to the top, isn't it," Chris whistled, "speaking to the royals and all?"

"Well, Virginia was a royal colony, and the explorations were done with the monarchy's blessing, so I'm sure they wanted to know what was going on over here, especially when it came to anything that would make them richer and more powerful," Harley explained.

"Okay, so this is written to Prince Charles. Please explain to us the significance," Abby remarked.

"Okay, first of all, the shape is what caught my eye. Chris, you said a V, and Abby, you said the text was centered. I say it's in the shape of a vortex... like a tornado." He paused for a moment, letting that sink in. Then he continued. "He asks God to bless him and prevent him from any accident that was beyond his power and reason to prevent. Well, I'd say a tornado would fit that category. What do you two think?"

Both Chris and Abby raised their eyebrows at this explanation. Harley recognized that both were beginning to understand the angle Harley was exploring. "Keep going," Chris encouraged.

"The rest of it sounds like Smith is asking to be rewarded handsomely for his actions, which if they include dealing with Atlantis, and, I know you two don't want to hear this, but the possibility of Atlantis being a cursed society, well, it begins to tie things together." Harley exhaled slowly after his lengthy oratory, waiting for some kind of rebuttal. It never came.

Instead, there was a short silence. Harley realized that he had actually left the other two speechless, and that it was very likely that everything he had just explained made complete sense to Chris and Abby.

Finally, Chris shook his head and exhaled loudly, "Whew! Harley, I don't know what to say except...I believe you. I mean, after all we have been through, this *does* make sense. I think you are on to something."

Abby reached over and squeezed his hand. "Harley, that's amazing! I think you're right too." She was beginning to become excited about Harley's discovery. "Anything else in there?"

"Yeah," Harley said, scrolling down the pages, "in two more of those dedicatory, they form the same shape. On is written to 'Lords, Knights and Gentlemen of his Majesties Council', and the other is written to 'Worshipful Adventurers for the Country of New England'."

"Do they have any more clues we could use?" Abby said, grabbing at Harley's phone. "Let me see!" She quickly snaked her hand toward Harley and yanked the phone out of his hand. Harley laughed at her eagerness.

Abby quickly scanned the other two entries.

Considering, with all, first those of his Maiesties Councell,
then those Cities aboue named, and diuerse
others that haue beene moued to lend their assistance
to so great a worke, doe expect (especially
the aduenturers) the true relation or euent
of my proceedings which I heare are so abused; I
am inforced for all these respects, rather to expose
my imbecillitie to contempt, by the testimonie
of these rude lines, then all should condemne
me for so bad a Factor, as could neither
giue reason nor account of
my actions and
designes.

Yours to command,
Iohn Smith.

She looked up and said in a hushed tone, "It sounds like he is hinting toward something huge, especially for the adventurers. Did you see that too, Harley?"

He nodded. "It sounds like he was saying many others had been involved in a huge endeavor, and that all of them should have been rewarded for their services, especially with all the inherent danger. Plus, it sounds like keeping all of this information under wraps had left his reputation in question. What do you think, Chris?"

Chris was peering over Abby's shoulder, studying the writing, as well as the shape. "I'd say you found something important, Harley, and now that you pointed that out, I think I found something too. I just didn't realize it at first, but now I think it is a huge deal."

It was Harley's turn to be left speechless. Finally he gasped, "What did you find?"

"I didn't think anything of it until you pointed out the vortex shape, but I found the same thing in William Bradford's *Of Plimoth Plantation*."

Harley could not believe what he was hearing, "As in William Bradford who lived across the street from Stephen Hopkins? As in one of the two men who were at Hopkins' deathbed and witnessed his will? Chris, please show me what you found!"

Chris pulled out his phone, punched in a few letters, waited a moment while it loaded, and then scrolled down the page. When he reached a certain point, he stopped, handed the phone to Harley, and commented, "What do you think?"

Abby, of course, jumped over to Harley and peered over his shoulder to see what Chris had found. They both immediately noticed a vortex shaped message that read:

Though I am growne aged, yet I have had a longing
desire, to see with my own eyes, something of
that most ancient language, and holy tongue,
in which the Law, and oracles of God were
write; and in which God, and angels, spake to
the holy patriarks, of old time; and what
names were given to things, from the
creation. And though I canot attaine
to much herein, yet I am refreshed,
to have seen some glimpse hereof;
(as Moses saw the Land
of canan afarr of) my aime
and desire is, to see how
the words, and phrases
lye in the holy texte;
and to dicerne somewhat
of the same
for my owne
contente.

J

Harley and Abby turned their heads and stared at Chris. They all seemed to grasp the magnitude of the discovery, leaving each one completely astounded and dumbstruck. Only the crackling of the fire could be heard as they continued to synthesize their findings.

"Oh, my God! Could this all be connected? Was the whole colonization of America just a conspiracy?" Abby was completely flabbergasted.

Harley, who had first been skeptical, then accepting of the existence of Atlantis, then terrified at the repercussions of a possible curse, was still taken aback by Chris' revelation. Anticipation and fear fought to surface first. He exhaled deeply, forcing down his own fears and doubts, and whispered, "Chris, you did it. This proves that others knew about it. Look at what it says."

Chris nodded, "I know."

Abby wanted a little more explanation. "What does it mean exactly? I get the gist of it, but the ancient language? Do they mean Greek?"

"Yes," Harley confirmed. "The Bible, God's Word, was written in Greek before it was translated into Latin, and then into everything else. It was during the Greek Empire. Hellenism is the term I learned in school. It was like a fusion of the Greek culture with all the Mideast cultures, which would have included the Jews. The Old Testament would have been translated into Greek."

Chris continued, "And it sounds like the writer was old, but had seen something akin to the Promised Land. Sounds like the writer was hoping for some sort of verification in the Bible, which is what I interpret the 'holy texts' to be."

Abby interrupted, "But if this is written by William Bradford, why does it have a J on the bottom?"

Chris explained, "I read the information prior to this passage, and this piece was actually written by Bradford's grandson Major John Bradford. It would seem that by simple extrapolation, Bradford may have shared info with his son, who in turn shared it with Bradford's grandson, John."

"Seems logical enough," Harley concluded, "although on the previous page it mentions the Hebrew language as well. Could we be missing something?"

Chris thought for a moment. "Harley, didn't you mention that most of the clues your mom, dad, and you found were written in a manner that required some interpretation? What I mean is that none of the other writings that were made public ever came straight out and said anything about Atlantis. You always had to read between the lines, right? Why would this be any different? Any unsuspecting person would read it as Hebrew, but we know that the Greeks would have been involved since we are considering it as a clue about Atlantis."

"And it does seem to fit with everything else we have found," Abby concluded. "I think we just found two more pieces of the puzzle verifying that something having to do with Atlantis is here in Plymouth. It just seems to make sense." She paused for a moment. "Now we just have to figure out what."

"Right," agreed Harley, "but as for tonight, I'd say we have done enough. It's getting late. Maybe it would be a good idea to sleep on what we've found and get a fresh start in the morning."

Chris nodded. "I'm pretty beat too. I think tomorrow is going to be a big day. I bet something occurs that will absolutely astound us, so I'm going to get a good night's sleep and be ready for it."

Chris had no idea just how precise his prediction was...but for all the wrong reasons.

<hr />

Their fourth day in Massachusetts began gloriously. As the sun rose into the air, there was a merry atmosphere around the campfire as the threesome prepared and devoured their breakfasts. All three were anticipating something of immeasurable assistance in their hunt for Atlantis.

After cleaning up, they decided that another trip into Plymouth would be the ideal plan. The strategy would be to widen their exploration of the town, visit with some of the locals who would have excellent background knowledge of the area, and gain an overall familiarity with the entire area that would have encapsulated Plimoth Plantation, including where the archaeological digs were being completed.

Chris drove them back downtown, parked the car near Pilgrim

Memorial State Park, and then the three explorers headed up the hill toward Main Street.

"Let's walk down Main Street to Samoset Street," suggested Abby. "Then we could walk up that and be sort of on the outskirts of where the plantation would have been."

"That's a little farther than the plantation spread, according to the map, but with it being named for Samoset, I'm for all the karma we can find," Chris intoned.

Harley agreed, "Right, and who's to say that what we are searching for would be in the plantation itself. Obviously the town grew, so trying to circle it, as it were, is probably a good idea."

"How far up do you think we should go?" Abby asked.

"Looking at the map, we could take it all the way up to Vine Cemetery, and then we could cut across," Harley explained. "Oak Grove Cemetery is basically connected to it, and from there we could head back toward the water on Summer Street. There's a walking path along Town Creek and Jenney Pond that looks like it would be kind of beautiful to hike." He smiled at Abby.

"Mr. Romance," she grinned. "Officer Chris," Abby continued coyly, "do you think I can trust this guy?" She turned to the police officer, who, being off duty, looked as much like a tourist as the others, all of whom were dressed in shorts and T-shirts.

Chris followed her lead, "Well, Miss Abby, he seems like an okay feller, but just you keep an eye on him and let me know if he gives you any trouble." He held up his prosthetic arm. "We pirates know how to handle scalawags. Arrrr!"

Harley and Abby burst out laughing. The mood could not have been any brighter as they made their way down Main Street, taking in the shops and view of the *Mayflower II*, bobbing gently in the small waves of the bay.

Once they made it to Samoset Street, they turned left, away from the bay, and began the steady ascent up the road, peering at both sides of the road for any piece of information that might give them a clue. They found nothing of any value, and finally made their way to the corner of Chestnut Street.

"Should we turn here and go in that entrance?" Abby pointed to the road that led off Chestnut and into the cemetery.

"Or we can cross here and go in the entrance off Samoset. That way we can just make our way across both cemeteries in one big swoop," Chris suggested. "We won't have to backtrack that way."

"Good thinking," Harley replied. "Let's do it."

They did just that, turning in off Samoset Street, and then meandering their way through the two cemeteries at a leisurely pace, searching for anything that might be helpful. It turned out that these particular cemeteries were begun well after colonial times, so there seemed to be little benefit in this particular expedition, other than admiring some of the headstones and memorials that stood in honor of those who had already passed on.

Still, it was an enjoyable time, racing from headstone to headstone, checking out dates, reveling at the age of some of them, and reminding themselves of all the sacrifices, especially the soldiers, had offered of themselves to insure a free and beautiful country.

"All gave some, and some gave all," Harley murmured at one point, while staring down at a grave of a Civil War soldier. "Makes you appreciate what little amount of time we have on this planet."

Chris and Abby both nodded silently, not needing to add anything to Harley's subtle reminder of all that had been lost in the last couple of years. As they stood quietly, a ringtone could be heard. "That's me," Chris stated, digging into his pocket to retrieve his cell phone. "Wonder who it could be? Hello?" he spoke into his phone. "Meghan? Uh, hi, this is a surprise. Is everything okay?" He glanced at Harley and Abby in surprise and shrugged his shoulders while he listened to the conversation on the other end of the line.

"Whoa! Hold on, Meghan. Slow down. Hang on just a second,

okay?" He placed his hand over the mouthpiece and motioned to the other two. "We're basically at the far end of the cemetery. There's Summer Street right there," he nodded in the direction of the road. "Why don't you two take that walk along Town Brook, and I'll meet you down on the other side by the bay. This," he nodded at the phone, "might take a little bit. Okay?"

Both Abby and Harley nodded, and Harley said quietly, "We'll give you some privacy, Chris. Take all the time you need. See you in a little while." He glanced up at the sky, which was beginning to cloud up with some slightly sinister looking thunderheads. "You might want to keep walking a little as you talk," he motioned toward the sky, "otherwise you might be in for a soaker before you get back down the hill. We'll stay out ahead of you."

"Thanks," Chris responded, nodding an affirmative to both the directions and the clouds that were beginning to pile on top of one another. "Okay, Meghan, now slow down and tell me what's going on. Start at the beginning."

"Let's go," Harley told Abby, gently taking her hand in his and leading her away from Chris and toward the exit of the cemetery. Once they reached the roadway, they crossed over, headed down Summer Street until they reached Billington Street. At that point Harley reversed his direction almost 180 degrees, as Billington nearly paralleled Summer at that point. It was only a couple of hundred yards and the two found the bridge that crossed Town Brook at that point.

"So, what do you suppose that is all about?" Abby asked, a troubled look on her otherwise striking appearance.

"I don't know," Harley replied. "Not sure if I should say anything, because Chris was kind of quiet about it, but he bought her a bracelet from the gift shop at Plimoth Plantation, kind of an expensive looking one, too."

"He did!" exclaimed Abby. "Why?"

"I think he's in love with her still. He said he was just going to give it to her as a Christmas present. I could see by the look on his face that he really cares about her, even if she did go and marry someone else."

"That's terrible, Harley," Abby lamented. "Chris is such a good guy. He deserves better."

"I can't disagree with you on that. I feel the same way."

They had reached the bridge and were crossing over. They stopped in the middle to take a couple of photos. Upstream was narrow, but downstream the brook widened into a pond.

"Is that the Jenney Pond you were talking about?" Abby asked.

"No, it's the next one down," Harley explained. "There's a path along the brook, and then it opens up again at Jenney Pond. From there it continues to the bay."

"So what's so special about Jenney Pond and Town Brook anyway?" asked Abby.

"Well, Town Brook was pretty much the salvation for the Pilgrims. It was their freshwater source. Without it, they would have been in some trouble. As for Jenney Pond, it was named after the Jenney Grist Mill. Supposedly the pond has lots of geese, swans, and ducks in it."

"So, not named after a girl named Jenny, then?" Abby queried.

"No, I guess not. I think it's named after John Jenney, who first made the grist mill back in the 1630s. It is actually something we can go tour, if you want. I guess it's one of the newer exhibits in the area. What do you think?"

"I guess we could do that, but we should probably meet up with Chris first, and then decide what to do," Abby finished.

"Well, let's keep walking then. He'll be along shortly."

They had reached the end of the first pond, and they proceeded to follow the trail along the brook until it broke out onto Willard Place, which was just a short street that ended in a circular turnaround at the end. From that point it was just a few short steps and they were once again crossing a bridge that spanned the waterway.

"There's Jenney Pond," Harley commented, stopping on the bridge and leaning over to stare at the water.

Sure enough, a number of waterfowl were swimming about, even some colorful male wood ducks.

"Sure is pretty," Abby commented dreamily, "and peaceful too."

"Almost as pretty as you," Harley added, "but not quite."

Abby turned away from the view, stared up at Harley, and to his surprise did not have a witty retort waiting for him. Instead she looked intently into his eyes and said softly, "Do you really think I'm that pretty?"

It wasn't in Harley's nature to ever deceive her, so he replied just as softly, "Yes, I think you are the most beautiful girl I've ever known."

Again, Abby's next response was not what Harley would have predicted. He had actually figured on receiving a kiss, but instead Abby just wrapped her arms tightly around his waist and buried her head in his chest. "Are you okay?" he asked her, gently caressing her golden hair.

"I guess so. I'm just worried about Chris, I guess." She pulled away ever so slightly and gazed up at him. "Just don't leave me. I don't want to think about you not being with me." Her eyes began to well up.

"Hey, hey, hey, what makes you even think that? Why would I want to be away from the best thing that has ever happened to me?"

"I don't know. I just get scared sometimes, I guess. You are the one person who knows me, better than anyone. I never have shared so much of myself with anyone, except maybe Anna, and she's gone, so please just don't ever let me go."

With that she again buried her head in his chest and squeezed him as if she was a vise. It was like a death grip, and Harley was momentarily stunned by the strength Abby was displaying. It nearly took his breath away.

Harley maintained control, and ever so gently stroked her hair over and over until he could feel the tension releasing itself from her arms. Finally she slowly released him from the embrace, reached up, placed her arms around his neck, and kissed him gently.

Harley smiled down at her. "Now that's what I was waiting for." He grinned crookedly at her.

The old Abby resurfaced immediately. She proceeded to glare at him and replied haughtily, "You're so pathetic, stealing kisses from girls who are feeling a little down. Better enjoy it, bud. You might not get another for a long time." With that she flounced down the bridge to the other side, her hair swinging from side to side, as Abby skipped the remaining few steps to the trail. At that point, she turned around and gave Harley that one smile that was reserved only for him, the one that she knew held him completely mesmerized.

"C'mon, lover boy, I want to see the rest of this Town Brook, and you're holding up the show. You're so slow sometimes. Might have to trade you in for another model," she teased.

"Coming, dear," Harley mocked, recalling that his mother and father used to verbally scrap with one another. His mother almost always won. "Like father, like son," he mumbled to himself. "Sometimes it's just worth it to lose."

"What are you grinning about?" Abby asked, as Harley joined her on the pathway.

"Oh, just thinking of my mom and dad, and how they would spar like this."

"And who would win?" Abby challenged.

"Who do you think? My mother, of course."

Abby smiled, "My mom, too. Guess it's just in the female DNA to put men in their place."

Harley just smiled and quipped, "Women. Can't beat 'em. May as well join 'em."

"Looks like your dad was a good teacher after all," she needled.

"The best," agreed Harley, who now glanced up at the sky. "Uh, it's starting to look ugly. Let's head down the path and find some shelter. I think we are in for a good drenching."

Abby glanced up as well, and a bolt of lightning streaked across the sky, followed momentarily by a booming thunderclap. They both jumped at the resounding rumble above their heads. For just a moment their eyes locked on one another. This time it wasn't out of affection. It was just plain fear. Harley saw the change in Abby's demeanor immediately, and he was certain she saw it in him as well.

"It can't be, Harley!" she cried out. "Please, God, tell me this is just a storm!"

Harley didn't answer. Instead he clutched Abby's hand and bolted down the path along the brook. He knew that if they reached Main Street, they could find shelter under the bridge that crossed over the waterway. They didn't make it that far. Instead they reached Market Street, and stopped under that bridge momentarily.

When no rain was forthcoming, Harley suggested, "Let's make a run over to the Main Street Bridge, and then we'll see what happens from there."

"Okay!" Abby replied, "Go!"

They sprinted the short distance to Main Street, reaching the cover of the overpass as the sky opened up with a fury. Lightning exploded across the sky. The thunder reverberated in their ears, causing the two teenagers to cover them in fear of burst eardrums. Torrents of rain deluged the city.

Harley had witnessed two tornadoes the previous year, but they had never come with such fury as he was witnessing. The tornadoes had been more of a surprise, dropping out of the sky without warning, and then disappearing almost as if they had been just a dream. This violent cloudburst continued to inundate the area with no signs of weakening.

Through the curtain of water that was pouring off the bridge to the ravine below, Harley could make out a figure sprinting toward them at full speed. Chris! He broke through the veil of liquid and into the small refuge that was the underpass.

"You two okay?" he shouted over the deafening sounds of the storm.

"We're fine," Abby shouted back, "but you look like a drowned rat!"

"Feel like one too, but guess what? You're not going to believe this! Meghan wants to see me. She wants us to get back together!"

"What?" Harley and Abby chorused.

"I know," Chris continued to shout. "It's unbelievable! She said she hadn't been happy in her marriage, and even though she didn't want to hurt anyone, she couldn't live her life as a lie anymore. She said she still loves me! Always has, always will! Can you believe it?"

"That's awesome, Chris! We were kind of worried that something was wrong, but it looks like everything is going to be great!" Harley shouted. "What did you tell her?"

"I was speechless at first, but then I told her I loved her too, and yes, I wanted her in my life. I told her where we are, and that she was welcome to come join us. You don't mind, do you?"

"No, that would be great, Chris! We'd love to meet her!" Harley yelled over the roar.

Abby called out, "That will be so awesome! I am so happy for you, Chris!"

"Thanks! Now all we have to do is wait for this cursed storm to get over, and then we can get some dry clothes."

It was as if a searing hot knife sliced into Harley's brain. Curse! Harley's moment of joy at Chris' good fortune now turned to absolute and utter fear and horror. The roar that had been the storm was now being eclipsed by another, more terrifying crashing noise. By the looks on the others faces, Harley knew they heard it too.

All three stared down at the water running alongside the path. They hadn't noticed how quickly it had risen, how it had completely covered the path and was rising rapidly. Too rapidly.

"Flash flood!" Chris shouted, "Go! Up the slope! Now!"

He shoved the two teenagers toward the downstream side of the bridge and out into the storm! It was now or never! Harley grabbed Abby's hand and pulled her toward the slope, slipping back down the embankment as the slick mud on the ravine's surface temporarily delayed their escape.

The crashing, grinding noise behind him alerted Harley, and as he peeked back, it was just long enough to see Chris, who was right behind him and shoving him forward with his good hand, slip back down toward to the water's edge. Chris was unable to use his prosthetic arm to maintain his balance, and he tumbled into the now raging waters that minutes before had been the peaceful Town Brook.

Harley watched helplessly as Chris surfaced momentarily, attempting to keep his head above the foaming, seething torrent. A downed tree swirled past, heading directly at Chris.

"Look out!" Harley screamed uselessly, his voice drowned by the deafening roar.

The log reached Chris in moments, and Chris, looking for anything that would support him, grabbed onto a branch. For a moment it appeared as if Chris would be out of harm's way, but then to the horror of his two friends on the slope of the now uncontrollable whitewater, the big log to which he was clinging suddenly jolted to a stop.

Because of the speed at which Chris had been swept away, the sudden lurch of the log flung him off the branch and back into the broiling water. Another log careening alongside Chris smashed into him and sent him under again. He didn't resurface.

And there, hanging gruesomely from the snagged log, was Chris's hook, dangling there as a reminder that, in one instant, another victim had fallen to the curse that was Atlantis.

The storm had abated in less than five minutes from the time Chris had disappeared under the water. Harley thought, "Just like Jamestown. Here and gone in a blink of an eye."

The two teenagers had scrambled up the slope and then sprinted down the short distance to where the brook emptied into the bay. There was no sign of Chris. Abby was the first to come to her senses. She pulled out her phone and dialed 911.

"Help!" she screamed into the phone. "We are by the bay where the brook empties into it. One of our friends got caught in a flash flood and we can't find him! Please hurry! Please, God, hurry!"

Abby slumped to the ground, dropped the phone, and began shrieking violently. "Nooooo! This can't be happening again! Not again! Not again!" She began bawling as if she was a lamb who had lost her mother. Her sobbing was ear-piercing, sending jolts of pain directly into Harley's spine and forever embedding them into his brain. It was as if God had forsaken them, leaving them to fend for themselves against unearthly forces.

Harley stood in frozen shock. No sounds came forth. He remained stock still for minutes, listening to the cries emanating from Abby's sprawled body. He could not go to her. He could not think rationally. It was as if his feet were fixed in cement. No cries. No tears. No emotion.

And then, slowly, seeping little by little from his subconscious, anger began to creep toward the surface. As it approached Harley's conscious thought, it turned to rage. Finally when the rage reached the surface, it became full flung fury.

He roared almost maniacally, shouting at the heavens, "What is wrong with you!? How can you do this to me? To us? What kind of God does this to anyone? I hate you! You are no God! You are nothing! You hear me? Come on! Why don't you try and take me? I'm right here! What more do you want from me? God only gives us what we can handle? That's bull! You're no merciful God! You're nothing but a cruel, spiteful God who doesn't give a damn about any of us!"

Harley's denouncement and vilification of his Creator left him spent, and he collapsed to the ground beside Abby. Meanwhile, Abby, who had been jolted out of her despondency by Harley's almost insane screaming, now stared at him in panic. She was transfixed by the outpouring of raw pain and emotion from the one person she trusted most, leaving her completely stunned and unable to move.

It was then that police, EMTs, and just ordinary citizens began piling toward them in a wave of humanity. Questions flew every which way until one of the officers took control of the situation and began a search and rescue operation starting at the Main Street Bridge all the way to the edge of the bay. The rescuers were hoping to have someone to save, but as Harley hunched over and began to vomit profusely, he knew there would be no one saved this day… physically or spiritually. Chris was dead.

————)((()))(————

The body wasn't found for almost 24 hours. It was quite possibly the worst 24 hours of Harley's life. First, he had to explain to the police who he and Abby were, as well as who Chris was, including the fact that he was a police officer visiting Plymouth from Virginia. Of course, that meant an immediate call down to the chief of Chris's department, the same chief that Harley has dealt with the previous year. He knew that the chief would suspect what the three had been up to, and he was not anticipating a happy reunion once they met again.

From what he could gather from the police in Plymouth, Chris's chief would be there the next morning. In the meantime, Harley and

Abby both had to call their grandmas and relay the horrible news. Because they were still minors, and Chris had the keys to the car, that left the two stranded and without adult supervision.

They informed the police of the situation, and once again they had to have a guardian placed in control of them until someone arrived to take care of them. Both Grandma Schultz and Grandma Larson told Harley and Abby that they would be flying out immediately.

The search continued all day, but to no avail. Harley and Abby stayed downtown until they were told by the police that they could return to the campground with an adult chaperone, and once both grandmas showed up, they were free to go.

The police in Plymouth had no doubt that this had just been a freak accident. It had just been a matter of being in the wrong place at the wrong time in a weather-related accident. There would not be a criminal investigation at all.

Unfortunately, Harley knew that they would not get away that easily once the chief from Virginia appeared. He would want to know all of the details surrounding the death, if Chris's body was ever found, as well as having to make arrangements for a funeral. Once again, it would be contingent on finding Chris.

Harley and Abby returned to the campground with the chaperone, and neither was in any mood to discuss anything. Harley was only vaguely aware of making a campfire and pulling out some food from their supplies. He had gone completely numb. Finally he just plopped down by the fire and stared at the flames. Abby, too, was lost in personal contemplation of the events that had transpired. The adult chaperone said little as well. It would be a long night.

Finally, they turned in, but Harley could not sleep. He continued to envision Chris being swept away and then submerging, never to surface again. Harley kept jolting awake when he would see the hook hanging off the branch. It replayed in his mind all night long. Like so many other events in the past couple of years, this was seared into his brain, never to fully leave.

Morning finally arrived, and Harley was again jolted awake, this time by the sound of his phone buzzing. He drowsily pulled himself to a sitting position and answered, "Hello?"

"Harley, this is the police chief in Plymouth. Sorry if I woke you, but I wanted you to know that we found your friend Chris."

Harley swallowed hard. "Where?" he croaked.

"His body washed ashore near the *Mayflower II*. I'm sorry, son."

Harley paused a moment. "Thank you. I appreciate it. Should we come down there?"

"Yes, I was just about to get to that. We need you to, um, identify Chris. Also, since you told me he had rented a car, we wanted to make sure you two could get his and any other personal possessions out of it before it was returned."

"I understand," Harley replied. "We'll be there as soon as we can."

"Okay, Harley, and once again, I'm sorry about your friend."

"Yep."

Harley clicked the phone. He took a deep breath and looked up at the top bunk. Abby was leaning over, peering down at him. She looked into his eyes, and then stated, "They found him, didn't they?"

Harley just nodded at her with a disconsolate look.

Abby whispered, "Guess we're supposed to go back into Plymouth, from the sound of your conversation. Sorry for eavesdropping."

Harley nodded again, and then he found his voice. "Yeah, I think I'll go clean up quick."

"Me, too," Abby replied, immediately pulling herself over the edge of the bunk and clambering down. Once she reached the floor, she reached out and grabbed Harley, in need of an embrace. They held each other for a few moments, and then they quietly gathered their toiletries and walked wordlessly to the showers.

A short while later they arrived at the police department. Much to Harley's mortification, the police chief from Virginia was already there, meeting the Plymouth police chief. When the chiefs saw Harley and Abby, they immediately motioned them toward an office where the four of them sat down around a table.

Chris's chief spoke first, "Well, Harley and Abby, seems we need to talk about a few things, yes?"

Harley and Abby glanced at each other and then back at the chief. "What would you like to know, Chief?" Harley asked.

"We," nodding at the other chief, "would just like for you two to explain the events from yesterday, so that we can have a clearer understanding of the events surrounding my officer's death."

"We already told our story yesterday. What else do you want to know?" Abby queried.

"That's true, but I would like to hear about it from you two personally, and then I would like to take a little trip over to the area where this all occurred."

Harley argued, "I thought we were here to identify Chris's body."

The chief shook his head. "No need. I took care of it already. It was Chris. I didn't think there was a need for you two to see that. I know that you three had become close. Chris would talk about you two every once in a while, so I just thought it would be better if you didn't see him in this...state," he finished sympathetically.

Harley and Abby appreciated the fact that neither would have to see Chris's body. They had enough of that the last couple of years. Harley was curious, however. "What is going to happen with Chris? I mean, what about a funeral?"

The chief nodded. "I understand. We have already contacted his family, and arrangements are being made to transport him back to Virginia, where he will be buried with honors."

"That's the least that should happen," Abby stated. "He saved our lives. We would have been killed also had he not acted so quickly."

"That's what I understand," the chief agreed, "and Chris will be recognized for his actions. That being said, I would still like an explanation, and I would like to head over to the scene. I realize that it was a horrific experience for you two, but I need to see for myself exactly what occurred. If you would be so kind as to accompany me, I'd like to do this now." It was more of a command than a question.

Harley retorted, "We're supposed to be waiting for our grandmothers. Shouldn't we stay here?"

The Plymouth chief, who had been listening to the conversation, nodded. "We have that all taken care of, Harley. I have a couple of patrolmen picking them up at the airport when they get in. You will be reunited with them as soon as they arrive. I promise you that. In the meantime, I think you should accompany Officer Newport's chief down to the site. He, and the officer's family, deserves a full explanation of the events that led to his passing. Your assistance would be very much appreciated."

Harley sighed. "Okay, let's get this over with." He and Abby stood up, and the two chiefs joined them.

The Plymouth chief said, "I'll stick around here and take care of paperwork, as well as wait for your family members. I'll contact the chief here," nodding at Chris's chief, "as soon as they arrive."

The two teenagers nodded. They were still none too happy at the prospect of retracing their steps from the previous day, but the chief was correct. The family did deserve to know the truth, especially how Chris had sacrificed himself attempting to save the others.

The three walked out to a police car, where the chief held the door open as they entered, slammed the door, and walked around to the other side, where he climbed in and started the engine. He had barely pulled out of the parking lot when he asked, "So do you two want to tell me what exactly you were doing here with Chris? My guess is that it once again has to do with Atlantis. Well?"

The two kids' silence affirmed what he suspected. He shook his head. "I would have thought by now that you two would have let this go. Seems to me every time you get involved, someone dies."

Both Harley and Abby started to protest, but he cut them off. "Okay, okay," he said hurriedly, "I didn't mean it as if it was your fault. You two don't control nature. I realize that, but all I'm saying is that it's an unfortunate coincidence that when you investigate this stuff, bad things tend to happen."

Neither of the two had an answer, so the chief continued. "How about you two explain where you were yesterday, and we'll find a good place to stop and then walk part of the way, okay?"

Harley was the first to answer, "That's fine, right Abby?"

"Sure, I guess so," Abby agreed, but it was none too enthusiastic.

Harley continued, "We actually walked up the north side of town to a couple of cemeteries. We were looking for historically significant tombstones from the time of the Pilgrims, but we didn't find any. When were almost through, Chris got a phone call from a woman named Meghan."

"Meghan?" the chief responded sharply. "What did she want?"

The two kids looked surprised at the chief's outburst. When neither responded right away, the chief continued, "Yes, I know who Meghan is, if you're wondering. Our police force is a tightly knit unit. We know a lot about each other, both professionally and personally. I know how much Chris cared, dare I say loved, that woman. So, I reiterate, do you know what she wanted?"

Harley glanced at Abby. She shrugged her shoulders and nodded. Harley took a deep breath and started, "Well, we didn't get the whole story, but the gist of it was that she wanted to get back together with Chris."

"What do you mean you didn't get the whole story?"

"Well, she called him while we were in the cemetery, so we went on ahead so he could have some privacy. He showed up just as the storm started, and he told us that she was getting divorced and wanted to know if she could see him again."

"You say you split up?"

"Yeah, at the cemetery."

"Then let's go there and walk the route from that point."

He punched in the cemetery location in the GPS, and it was just a short ride until they reached the far end where Chris had remained behind, and Harley and Abby had taken their stroll alongside the brook. The chief pulled the car over, the three exited the vehicle, and Abby pointed, "Right there is where we came out of the cemetery. We started walking down the street here, and then we picked up the trail over by the stream."

"Let's go then," the chief directed.

Harley could not believe he was retracing this route not even 24 hours after the loss of his friend. It had been such a beautiful day, walking and talking with Abby. How could such a wonderful day have ended so terribly?

They crossed over the first bridge and picked up the trail. As they walked, the chief asked, "What was it you thought you would find here?"

"Nothing in particular," Harley commented.

"So am I to assume that you were searching for information relating to the previous Atlantis discoveries you and your family made?" When neither answered he continued, "A lack of an answer pretty much tells me that the answer is yes. Do you mind telling me what even led you to Plymouth in the first place?"

Still no answer. He sighed, "Well, there's no law in keeping secrets, unless, of course, it is something illegal. Since there is nothing unlawful about searching for past historical events, I guess there's little I can do to convince you to share your findings. However, based on all you've found so far, and the bizarre events surrounding all of it, you might be better off telling *someone* what's going on, just to be on the safe side."

His plea for more information fell on deaf ears. Neither Harley nor Abby was in a particularly sharing mood, especially as they realized they were almost to the bridge where they had run for cover from the monster storm from the previous day.

All along the path and the brook lay remnants of trees, branches, and other debris that the flash flood had carried downstream. As Harley studied the area, a thought occurred to him. "What do you mean by bizarre?"

The chief replied, "That flash flood yesterday was the first recorded here. They have never seen such a deluge in such a short amount of time. It was unprecedented."

With that confirmation, Harley now understood that it wasn't a matter of wrong place, wrong time. He had long given up on coincidences. The word *curse* was no longer just a possibility, as far as he was concerned. It was a reality. Somehow, in some way, attempting to solve the mystery of Atlantis was plagued with affliction. He could no longer ignore all the signs. Still, he had made a promise to his mother that he would find out the truth. His brain and heart were in a conflict-ridden turmoil.

Fortunately, he was unable to rummage through his thoughts for very long because they had arrived at the bridge. He and Abby stopped just before crossing that particular threshold. The chief pulled up and stared at them. "Well, why are you stopping?"

Abby pointed, "That's where we were standing when Chris showed up. I'm not sure I want to go back under there."

The chief nodded. "I understand, Abby. Let's talk right here for a minute. Just tell me if I have this right. You two were standing under the bridge, trying to stay out of the storm, when Chris came running down to you. Right?"

Harley and Abby nodded their assent.

The chief continued, "So then while you were under there, he told you about his conversation with Meghan?"

They nodded again.

"Could you please tell me what he said? I'm sure I will be seeing

Meghan at some point. It would be nice to be able to offer some kind words at least."

Harley answered, "Chris only had time to tell us that Meghan was extremely unhappy without him, that he loved her, and that he had invited her to come and join us. Oh, God, she's coming here! How are we supposed to tell her about this? The fact that she feared he might be killed in the line of duty was the reason they broke it off in the first place."

The chief nodded. "I knew that. Chris told me that once. Let's return to yesterday's events. What else did he say?"

Abby answered, "That was it. It was about then that we looked down and noticed that the water level had reached our feet, and there was this loud, roaring sound. Chris knew it was a flash flood, and he yelled at us to go out the other side of the bridge and climb up the embankment."

The chief shook his head. "Okay, got it. I'm going to ask you to come with me even though I know you don't really want to go through with this. Let's walk under the bridge and you can show me where you tried to go up the side of the stream. I promise I won't make you stay long."

Harley and Abby reluctantly followed him under the bridge, and true to his word, he didn't even stop underneath, but continued back out into the sunshine. Once he was a few yards beyond, he stopped and looked up the embankment. Then he peered at Harley and Abby.

Abby said, "That's where we tried to go up the slope, but we kept slipping. I was in the front, Harley was behind me, and Chris was pushing us along as best as he could. He slipped back and fell into the water."

Harley continued, "We saw him come up once, but then a log hit him, and he grabbed onto a branch. Whatever log he was hanging onto stopped suddenly, and then his," Harley paused for a moment, "his hook came off, and he disappeared.

Harley pointed downstream to the very tree Chris had clung to so desperately. It had become hung up by other logs that had been under the waterline. Much to Harley's relief, the hooked arm no longer hung from one of the branches.

The chief must have read Harley's thoughts. "Some searchers found his prosthesis during the search. The search actually started from that point, or so I was told." He took a deep breath. "Okay, you two, I want to thank you for doing this for me. It really does help me understand what happened. Let's head up to the road and retrace our steps to the car. We don't need to walk back the way we came."

Harley and Abby were quietly grateful for that. Both knew that the chief was just doing his job, and that the next few days would be difficult for him as well. He had lost an officer, and from the sounds of it, quite possibly a friend. That realization made Harley ask, "Chief, how well did you know Chris?"

The chief answered a little gruffly, "We were partners when Chris first came on board. We got to know each other very well. That's why I know so much about Meghan."

Harley and Abby stared at him, dumbfounded. Neither had any idea how personally this had affected this man. It was obvious that he was hurting too. As a professional, he was doing his job as efficiently and skillfully as one would expect from a police officer. As a human being who had just lost a friend, and he just wanted answers, to make sense of this whole tragedy.

Abby responded, "We're sorry for your loss, Chief. We didn't know that you two were that close."

Harley added, "Yeah, we're sorry. I'm sure it's not going to be easy for any of us for the next few days."

The chief responded with a sigh, "At least he died trying to help others survive. That, in and of itself, was the heart of Chris's whole being. His family needs to know about it, and he needs to be honored in some way."

Abby quietly added, "He always will be our hero. He saved us, plain and simple."

The rest of the return trip to the car was walked in silence, as each individual struggled with their own thoughts. When they reached the car, Harley's phone buzzed. It was his grandma.

"Hey, Grandma."

"Harley, where are you?"

"I'm just downtown with Chris's chief. We were just showing him what happened. We are heading back to the station right now. Be there in a few minutes."

"Okay, then I'll see you soon. Abby's grandma is here too, so we can take care of things when you arrive."

"Okay, Grandma, see you in a little bit."

He clicked his phone off, and then he realized something. "Chief, what about the rental car?"

The chief replied, "I have the key. It was recovered by the searchers, as well as his other personal possessions. What do you need?"

"Well, we have a couple of personal possessions in it, and I think Chris may have had some stuff in there as well."

"Let's run down there quick, and you can grab your things."

Once they reached the rental car, the chief unlocked the doors and trunk. Harley and Abby retrieved some souvenirs and a couple of sweatshirts, and then Harley opened the glove compartment. There, still in the little bag from Plimoth Plantation, was the bracelet that Chris had purchased for Meghan. He deftly grabbed it and placed it in his pocket. As soon as he saw it, he knew he owed it to Chris to personally deliver the gift, along with an explanation.

"Got everything?" the chief asked.

"I think so," Harley replied. "What about you, Abby?"

Abby said, "Yeah, I don't see anything else." She had seen Harley grab the small package, and she looked at him quizzically.

Harley shook his head almost imperceptibly, hoping that Abby would let it go for the time being. He would explain later. Abby seemed to understand, nodded, and then called out to the chief, "I guess we're ready to go. You can lock it up."

The chief clicked the button on the key fob, and the alarm chirped. He placed the keys in his pocket, and then said, "Okay, let's head back to the police station. Your grandmothers will be there, and I want to get a hold of Meghan, if possible. I'm afraid it won't be pretty when she finds out."

The chief could not have been more accurate with his prediction.

———— ((O)) ————

When they arrived back at the police station, both grandmas were waiting. The chief motioned toward them, and told Harley that he was going to contact Meghan and Chris's parents. Abby rushed into Grandma Larson's arms and she burst out crying. Harley accepted Grandma Schultz's embrace, but he was too numb to speak, too void of emotion to even comprehend what was going on around him.

"Oh, Harley," Grandma Schultz started, "I am so sorry about Chris. He was a fine young man. I know how much you liked him, and how much he meant to you."

"Thanks, Grandma." Harley stated, almost robotically. "He saved my life…twice. Look what it got him." There was complete bitterness in his voice.

Grandma Schultz heard his tone, pulled away for a moment, and looked into his eyes. What she saw startled her. A face that normally was full of life and determination, one of stubborn doggedness, now had a look of defeat and, worse, a look of rage and wanton vengeance.

She had never seen that look on her grandson's face, even when he had buried his mother, after Anna's death, or even after his father's demise. Harley had taken the losses as anyone else would. There was some anger, some depression, and then acceptance. This time was different. His entire demeanor had changed. He was almost a different person.

Grandma Schultz decided on another course of action. She squeezed Harley's arm and walked over to Abby. Grandma Larson released Abby, allowing Grandma Schultz the opportunity to embrace the hurting young woman. Grandma Larson, in turn, came over to Harley and placed her arms around him.

Grandma Schultz offered her condolences to Abby, and then very quietly asked her, "Abby, Harley seems very different. Can you tell me what happened?"

She nodded and whispered, "Grandma, he scared me. He was screaming at God and almost daring God to kill him too. I've never seen him like that. I was actually afraid for a minute."

Grandma Schultz pulled Abby back into her embrace and soothingly whispered, "It's okay, Abby. Thank you for telling me. We'll work through this together. I promise."

Glancing up at Harley, she hoped that she could keep that promise. He stood there statue-like, just staring out into space. This was not going to be easy.

A commotion in the doorway grabbed all their attention. A very pretty young woman burst through the doorway, a wild look in her eyes. She scanned the room, searching for any familiar face. Chris's chief walked out of one of the offices and approached her. "Meghan," he called.

"Chief?" The woman had a look of astonishment on her face as she took in the familiar figure. "What are you doing in Plymouth? Why did the police escort me here? What's going on?"

The surprised look on her face began to change to one of fear as the chief took her arm gently and motioned to the same office where Harley and Abby had spoken with him earlier in the day. "Let's go talk for a minute, Meghan."

The pair slowly made their way into the small room. Harley

watched through the glass, knowing what was coming. It didn't take long. A scream of anguish reverberated through the station, as the realization of Chris's death set in. Harley felt the screams right down to the core of his being. "No! No! No!" A continuous shriek of disbelief echoed in his ears.

Finally, Meghan was able to calm down enough for the chief to explain the events of the past 24 hours. Harley could see her sobbing as the chief tried to console her.

Then at one point during the chief's explanation, Harley saw her turn her head and gaze directly at him, and momentarily at Abby. The stare then returned to him. Slowly she stood up, her eyes never leaving Harley. She glowered at him as she pulled open the door and began marching quickly toward him.

"Meghan!" The chief called out, attempting to catch up with her.

Harley held up one hand to the chief and called out to him, "Let her go, Chief."

Meghan had reached Harley. The two grandmas and Abby had inched away, waiting to see what would become of this confrontation. Meghan exploded. "You!" she screamed. "You just couldn't let it go, could you? You had to keep pushing! You had to keep digging! Wasn't it enough that he lost his arm because of you? Now you got him killed! I hate you! I wish you were dead! You have wrecked everything! How many more have to die before you're going to stop?"

With that final denouncement, Meghan clenched her fist, cocked her arm, and swung with all of the power she could muster, straight at Harley's chin. Harley saw it coming, knew it was coming, but refused to make any effort to defend himself. Crack! Meghan's fist struck home. Harley's head snapped back, and he staggered back one step, but regained his balance.

Plymouth policemen and Chris's chief all surged forward to stop her, but again Harley held up his hand. "No! Let her go!"

Meghan was overcome with grief and anger combined. She

fell into Harley and pounded on his chest again and again, doing little damage to Harley physically, but absolutely devastating him emotionally and spiritually. Finally, she collapsed on the floor at his feet. She lay in a heap, sobbing. A policeman came over to Harley, handed him a couple of tissues, and pointed to Harley's lip. Meghan's blow to his face had caused a cut.

Harley took the tissue, completely unaware of any pain, and placed it up to his face. Then he just stared down at the forlorn figure situated on the tile floor. The station was completely silent as the rest of the people in the police station watched and waited.

After what seemed like an eternity, Meghan gathered herself together and slowly rose to her feet. She locked eyes with Harley, but there was little or no regret in them for what she had done. Harley could see that there would never be forgiveness forthcoming. He also saw in her gaze that she would never forgive herself for not marrying Chris and at least having spent a few years together. The regret was obvious.

Harley never lowered his gaze, but he slowly reached into his pocket and pulled out the little bag that contained the bracelet that Chris had purchased for Meghan at Plimoth Plantation. He slowly held it out toward Meghan and murmured, "Chris bought this for you the other day. He said he wanted to give it to you for Christmas. He said he was still in love with you. Then you called, and I never saw him happier."

Meghan slowly took the bag from Harley and opened it. As she pulled the bracelet out, she cried out again, holding it up to her opposite wrist. There, dangling and sparkling in the light of the room, was another bracelet. It was eerily similar to the one from the bag. While it had a different design, the type of stones was the same.

"He gave me this bracelet as a promise that he would love me forever!" she wailed, pointing to her wrist.

"He did," Harley stated simply. "He surely did."

And with that statement Harley turned away and strode out of the police station, leaving the entire group standing there in disbelief.

———————————

"Harley, wait!" Abby rushed outside, attempting to catch Harley as he marched away from the police station. "Where are you going?"

Harley stopped momentarily, turned around to stare at Abby, and then grunted, "I just need some space. Tell my grandma that I will meet her back here in a while. I have my cell."

Abby protested, "Let me come with you."

"No, just stay away from me."

Abby stepped back as if she had been slapped. Harley had never spoken to her in that tone ever before, and it frightened her. He turned away and began jogging away from the station.

Grandma Larson and Grandma Schultz had made it outside in time to see Harley turn the corner and disappear from view. "Where's he going, Abby?" Grandma Schultz asked quickly.

Abby turned around to face the two grandmothers, her eyes welling up with tears. "I don't know! He said he'd come back in a while, but he told me to stay away from him. I've never heard him talk like that, Grandma Schultz, and it scares me. I'm afraid of what he might do!"

Grandma frowned at that statement, but she consoled Abby, "It'll be okay, Abby. He just needs some space. That was a pretty intense confrontation back there. Let's give him some time."

Abby shook her head. "No, Grandma, it's more than that. I could tell by the look in his eye and the tone of his voice. Something has happened to him, something bad. I just know it."

Grandma took a deep breath. "Okay, Abby, let's just give him a few minutes, and then I will call him and check to make sure he's okay, all right?"

Abby couldn't trust her voice, so she simply nodded.

Meanwhile, Harley set off at a jog toward downtown Plymouth, which was a little less than two miles from the police station. As he ran, his chaotic thoughts left him in complete disarray. The more he thought, the harder he ran. Soon he was sprinting in an attempt to rid himself of the demons that were eating away at his subconscious.

In a matter of minutes he found himself on Main Street, crossing over the very bridge he had been hiding under with Abby, the bridge above where his friend Chris had been swept away before his eyes. He didn't even slow down, and he continued to Leyden Street, at which point something drew him back up the street to Burial Hill.

He finally stopped to catch his breath at the entrance. He continued inside and, huffing and puffing, made his way up to William Bradford's headstone. From there he turned and looked out over the bay. Once he caught his breath he looked around.

Much to his surprise, many of the headstones were no longer upright. Instead he noticed that a number of them, especially those on sharper slopes had been washed away down the hill. Obviously, the flash flood had not only taken Chris, but it had done damage throughout the city. Apparently the graveyard wasn't a priority for cleanup.

Harley leaned against Bradford's headstone, and he was completely startled when the headstone began to topple. He barely caught his balance as the large monument tumbled over. "Oh, my God, can anything else go wrong?"

He walked around the downed stone marker, wondering if he could find a way to right the extremely heavy weight. Coming up blank in that regard, he walked around to the base and glanced down into the deep impression that the marker had left in the earth.

He half expected something to be there waiting for him, another clue that would keep him absorbed in the search for Atlantis. The logical part of his brain knew that the monument had not been placed there until the 1800s, although there was some debate about the actual year. When nothing met his eye, he gave an audible sigh of relief.

"Good, as if I needed anymore hassle."

He began working his way through the cemetery, assessing the damage from the storm, and deciding that he could at least inform the police chief of Plymouth that there had been damage at the cemetery, when he came to an extremely steep part of the cemetery.

A couple of stones had fallen over, and a groove had been cut in the side of the hill, enabling the force of the water to erode away the bank. The force must have been that of a bulldozer because the huge groove, not unlike the one that occurred at Jamestown during the first tornado, had exposed the earth to a depth of six feet or more in some places.

The next thing Harley noted had him gulping for air. Bones were scattered around the vicinity. A couple of old wooden caskets had been unearthed, and now the remains were left drying in the sun. Harley shivered at the sight. "Not again," he muttered.

Against his better judgment, almost drawn by external forces, Harley began to investigate the area. Part of his brain, the logical side, screamed at him to leave immediately, to let it go. The other part of his brain, the inquisitive side, continued the search. It did not take long until he found what he was looking for, what he dreaded and anticipated all at once. It was no coincidence that he had made his way here. It was fate. Right then and there, Harley knew he would have to complete this quest one way or another. It was as if he had been predestined.

There, staring at him among the skeletal remains, lay another leather parcel, sealed from the weather for centuries, now split apart, with an old parchment peeking out from under the flap. Harley could not help but to be drawn toward it, and he slowly, carefully reached down and retrieved the little bundle.

Gingerly, he opened the flap and cautiously removed the paper. He unfolded it, and there it was, the clue he had hoped to find, the clue he dreaded he would find. It was the final clue he needed.

His first glance was at the signature. The name of Stephen Hopkins stared up at him from the page. Harley shook his head at the connections his father must have made between Jamestown and Plymouth, and how he had included them in his notes. "Well done, Dad. You gave me enough information to lead me to the right place. I still don't know exactly what you were trying to say to me, but at least your notes are dead on. Now it's just a matter of figuring out what Hopkins is trying to say."

The words were in an odd shape, neither a spiral, which the first amulet and the hurricanes were, or a vortex, as the second amulet, the tornado, John Smith's note, and Major Bradford's note all were shaped. Harley didn't grasp the shape right away, so instead he studied the message.

Thus trusting in the Lord that
the true meaneing of said discoveries may
one day be revealed, the final talisman has thus beene
bequeathed to the sea, being a strange and wonderfull
occurrence whereas the sea itself has fallen away and the land
exposed such a bolder that wouldst keep the secret secure
until such time as wee may discover said truths.
May the Lord direct you herein to eternity.

Stephen Hopkins

Harley reread the message numerous times, struggling to comprehend the meaning behind the message. One realization did set in rather quickly however. "There's a third amulet! Hopkins knew that Smith had buried the second with Gosnold, and that the first was somewhere at Roanoke. He must have hidden it here somewhere. But why?"

He stared at the message again. "What does he mean by the sea has fallen away? That doesn't make sense. Low tide maybe, but if some boulder was exposed, then why wouldn't we be able to see it now?"

Harley took a deep breath. He knew he should take this incredible find to the authorities, but he was torn once again by his desire to see this quest all the way to the end, to fulfill the promise he had made to his mom. If he gave all this information up, he knew that there would be a massive search in the harbor for this rock, or boulder, or whatever it was that held quite possibly the final clue to finding Atlantis.

Another part of his mind began to process the possibility that continuing this search could ultimately lead to more death and destruction. Before he had time to delve into that possibility, his phone buzzed.

"Hey, Grandma. Yes, I'm fine. I was just about ready to head back. I'm in downtown Plymouth. I can meet you either at the police station or down by Plymouth Rock. Okay, I'll see you in a few minutes down by the bay."

He clicked his phone off, stuffed it into his pocket, and then placed the leather pouch and letter under his shirt and kept it held in place by his belt and waistband. Then he started trotting back down the hill on Leyden Street and arrived near Pilgrim Memorial State Park in just a couple of minutes.

There was no sign of his grandma yet, so he took a stroll down near the water's edge, staring out over the water and wondering what lay beneath the waves. "Wait until I tell Abby!"

It was then that trepidation clutched him, causing him to gasp out, "No, I can never tell her about this! Everyone else who knew about this has died. She can never know. I have to keep her away from this, no matter what."

Harley turned his eyes toward the sky, "You've taken every single person I cared about, anyone that was involved in this. First Mom, then Anna and Marlene, next Dad, and now Chris. I will *never* let you hurt Abby, even if I have to give her up myself. You hear me? You will not take *her* from me. You will not take *anyone* from me. *Ever again!*"

With that vow, he turned away from the sea and headed to the parking lot. Grandma was in a car, waiting for him. Grandma Larson and Abby were in the car as well. Harley took a deep breath. This was going to turn ugly in a hurry, but he was not about to lose anyone else. He had made his decision. He and Abby would be no more.

⸺⸺»《●》«⸺⸺

"Harley, think about what you are saying. You cannot be serious about breaking off your relationship with Abby because of what has happened to Chris." Grandma Schultz had barely closed the door to the hotel room where they were now staying.

After picking him up in Plymouth, they had driven to the campground, gathered their possessions, and had spoken to the campground owners about the situation. The owners had no problem refunding their remaining stay, as the circumstances dictated a great degree of tactfulness.

From there they had found a motel in Plymouth that would keep them near downtown. Harley spoke nary a word all the way to the campground and all the way back to the motel. The two grandmas attempted to exchange some pleasantries and small talk, but soon they fell silent as well. It was a very steep precipice on which they were teetering, and both realized that two teenagers' lives hung in the balance.

When they reached the motel, Harley wasted little time in making a decision. "Grandma, I would like to go home as soon as possible, tonight or tomorrow."

"Harley, don't you want to see about the funeral arrangements for Chris? I'm sure his chief would be more than accommodating and keep us in the loop. He seems like a fine man, and I'm sure we could just get a rental car or fly down to Virginia from here. Plus, I think it would do some good to see his parents, don't you?"

"No, I don't. I'm not going to another funeral. I'm sick of people dying. I'm sick of disaster following me wherever I go. I'm sick of it all. I just want to go home." His voice was dripping with animosity.

Abby, who had done her best to control her emotions for the past half an hour, said quietly, "Harley, please don't do this. Chris was our friend. We should be at the funeral."

"You go then. I'm done with this, done with everything."

Abby's eyes grew wide. "What do you mean by everything? Does that include me?"

Harley looked her dead in the eyes and declared, "Yes, it means you, too."

Abby looked as if she had just been slapped in the face. "You can't mean that?"

"Well, let's see," Harley began bitterly, "your uncle killed my mother, and then tried to kill my dad and me. He wasn't successful there, but he was able to kill off Anna and her mom and dad. Then your parents tried to kill my dad and me, and even if they didn't actually pull the trigger, they were in part responsible for my dad's death. Now I'm here with you, and Chris dies. Maybe Meghan should have punched you in the face. Maybe you and your family are the cause of all this disaster!"

Abby was completely bowled over by this lashing out by Harley. She had seen how upset he had been when they realized Chris had died. Still, this outburst left her stunned and speechless. Harley gave her no chance to respond. He quickly spun away and stomped to his room, opened the door, and slammed it behind him.

Both Grandma Larson and Grandma Schultz tried to console a distraught Abby, who immediately slumped down to the ground, completely shocked and emotionally spent from all that had occurred. She sobbed hysterically for what seemed hours. She was hyperventilating at times, and both grandmothers began to consider taking her to the hospital and get her something that would calm her down.

Finally, Abby was able to catch her breath and compose herself. As her breathing calmed, Grandma Schultz spoke softly to her, as well as to Grandma Larson, "I apologize for Harley's words. Even though he is hurting too, he had no call to lash out at you. You did nothing wrong. I hope that you will find it in your heart to forgive him. I know he cares about you, Abby. Daresay, I think he is in love with you."

"Funny way to show it," Grandma Larson remarked quietly.

Grandma Schultz had to concede that point. She nodded and replied, "Abby, will you be okay for a little bit with your grandmother?"

Abby nodded.

"Okay, I need to go speak with my grandson," she said harshly. Her voice softened. "I want you to know that I, we, care about you very much. I am so sorry that all of this has happened to you. You are a sweetheart, and the best thing to ever happen to that young man." She straightened up. "I am going to see to it that he apologizes to you, and hopefully you will be able to forgive him. We'll see you a little later, okay?"

"Thanks, Grandma Schultz, I appreciate all you've done," Abby whispered.

The two grandmothers exchanged concerned, if not hardened, glances. Grandma Schultz nodded another apology and headed for the motel room to confront her grandson.

Meanwhile, Harley sat on the edge of the bed, hardly believing the vile filth he had spewed at Abby. How could he be such a jerk?

His parents had always taught him to be a gentleman, and here he had gone overboard in the other direction. He tried to reason with himself that it was all for the best, that he had to sacrifice his relationship with Abby to keep her safe. That was all there was to it.

When the brain fights the heart, there is no winner. Harley tried to rationalize what he had done, but inside he was completely broken. He buried his face in the pillow and screamed. The sound was muffled enough that no one heard him, but he did realize that he would need to compose himself and remain steadfast in his decisions once Grandma set foot inside.

She was a force to be reckoned with, and he understood that she was going to make him apologize, and also try to persuade him to go to the funeral. He would relent on the former, but he would not cave in on the latter. He needed to make a clean break with Abby. Anything less and neither would be able to ever move on.

There was a gentle knock on the door, and then his grandmother unlocked the door with her pass key. She walked over to the other bed in the room, sat down, took a deep breath, and quietly started, "Well, that was certainly interesting."

Harley said nothing, but instead just stared at the floor. Grandma continued, "Harley, think about what you are saying. You cannot be serious about breaking off your relationship with Abby because of what had happened to Chris."

This was it, Harley thought. It was now or never. "I am serious, Grandma. I want to go home. Now! I don't ever want to see this place again, or have anything to do with any part of it."

Grandma sighed. "Okay, Harley, I will not argue with you about staying or going. We'll take the first flight back to Michigan that we can find."

"Thank you, Grandma."

"I'm not finished, young man. You said some very hurtful things to that young lady out there. Now, I think you are wrong about breaking things off with her, but it is your life, not mine. I think she is the best thing that ever happened to you, and that is my opinion. That being said, you owe her an apology for the things you said, whether you meant them or not. You were not raised that way. So," she concluded, "as soon as you take care of that, I will take care of our flight plans."

"Okay, Grandma." Harley stood up and readied himself for what would be the most difficult task of his young life. He was about to tell the girl he had fallen in love with that it was over. He shook his head and headed for the door, but Grandma stopped him.

"Give your old grandma a hug."

Harley nearly lost it right there, but somehow he retained his composure. He squeezed her for a moment, and then exited the room.

The irony of Chris's and Meghan's situation had not gone unnoticed either. Meghan had backed out of the relationship for fear of losing Chris, and now Harley was doing the same thing. He muttered under his breath, "And when she tried to get him back, he died. The very thing she feared had happened. Well, it's not going to happen to me."

With that thought, his resolve returned, and he walked over to Abby's room. He knocked gently. Grandma Larson opened the door, nodded at Harley, and asked, "Would you like to speak to Abby?"

"Yes, Grandma Larson, if she wants to hear me."

"Abby," she called, "Harley is here."

Abby came to the door. Her eyes were red and slightly swollen. Despite that, Harley could still not believe just how beautiful she was. For a moment he wavered. She looked at him without saying a word, but he could see in her demeanor that she was now on the defensive. A wall had been built.

Harley cleared his throat. "I just wanted to say I'm sorry for the things I said about your family. I know they are not true. I have no excuse for my behavior. Grandma Larson, I apologize to you as well.

You should not have had to hear those things either."

Abby said nothing. She just stood there, staring. Harley could not meet her gaze. Grandma Larson broke the silence. "Very well, Harley, we accept your apology. It may take a little bit for us to forget, but we do know how to forgive. Isn't that right, Abby?"

Abby had not taken her eyes from Harley. She didn't answer, but simply nodded. Her lower lip quivered. She was not going to cry in front of Harley, no matter what became of the situation. Harley only glanced at her long enough to catch the nod, returned the nod, and then said, "Well, I guess I better go back to my grandma. We have to make arrangements to leave."

Grandma Larson responded, "May I ask what arrangements you will be making?"

"We're going back to Michigan." Harley was still staring at the carpet.

"And the funeral?"

Harley didn't trust his voice. He simply shook his head.

"And me?" Abby breathed, her voice barely audible.

Harley paused a moment, then shook his head. He turned away and closed the door behind him. It was over. It was all over.

Prologue

(Revisited)

"JOSEPH SCANTON," THE principal intoned.

A few scatterings of applause jerked Harley back into the moment. He was next. He was going to officially graduate high school. The moment was bittersweet. No mom, no dad, no Anna, no Abby.

"Harley Schultz," the principal called.

Harley slowly began the walk over to the principal. Loud murmurs were obvious throughout the crowd. Everyone knew about him, about his family, about Atlantis, about Chris. No cheers or wolf whistles. No polite applause. Just the murmurings.

Harley clenched his jaw tightly. "That's right, go ahead and judge me," he thought. "None of you have a clue what I've been through, except what has been sensationalized in the papers."

He had reached the principal. "Congratulations, Harley," he said. "Best wishes to you in your future endeavors."

"Thank you," was Harley's noncommittal reply.

He proceeded down the other side of the stage, and there was Grandma Schultz, Uncle Ron, Aunt Linda, and all of his relatives from both Michigan and Wisconsin. Many were attempting to grab his attention so they could snap a photo. He did his best to smile, but his heart wasn't in it.

The rest of the ceremony passed by quickly, and soon he found himself out in the commons, surrounded by family, all jabbering on about what a wonderful graduation program it had been. Then came the inevitable photo shoots. Some of his teammates from his baseball, basketball, and football squads asked him to join in some of the shots.

Harley was indifferent to the whole situation, so rather than cause any kind of scene at all, he simply complied and smiled politely for anyone who asked for a picture.

After a little while, the crowd had thinned, and Grandma Schultz took charge. "Okay, the graduation party begins in about an hour, so let's head out and get home before the guests arrive."

Harley was more than ready to go. He held up the keys to the car. "Want me to drive you, Grandma?"

She nodded. "Let's go."

The ride back to the house was only about 10 minutes, but it was enough time for Grandma to have a heart to heart discussion with him.

They had barely pulled out of the parking lot when she started speaking. "Harley, Abby called to wish you a happy graduation."

Harley nodded, not willing to speak about Abby. He had not spoken her name for almost a year now, but despite that, she was maddeningly in his thoughts and dreams on a daily, and nightly, basis.

Grandma tried again. "Do you think you could email or text her? She graduates tomorrow. I think she would appreciate some kind of acknowledgment."

Harley sighed. "I don't think so, Grandma. It's just better this way."

Grandma harrumphed. "Better for whom? I haven't heard you laugh for so long, and you seldom smile. Grandma Larson said that Abby is in a funk too. She went through her senior year with no enthusiasm at all. That's just not right, Harley. Now, be honest with me, do you still care for the girl?"

"Doesn't matter either way, Grandma. What's done is done. There's no going back now."

"I'll agree to disagree with you on that one," she responded. "It's never too late."

"It is as far as I'm concerned."

"Okay, Harley, I'll give it a rest. Now, you are a high school graduate, with honors I might add. Well done. You've been accepted to the University of Michigan, just as you had hoped. You have the summer ahead of you. Any plans?"

Harley thought for a moment. He did have some plans, but he was unsure if he would be allowed. Still, his 18th birthday was in just a few days, so he could legally do what he wanted. He was wary of alienating his family, as he had been less than cordial over the past year, choosing to avoid family outings in Michigan or Wisconsin.

"Well, I turn 18 soon, and even though I wouldn't actually need permission, I'm still asking you if it would be okay to take my bike on a trip."

"Where would you go?" Grandma asked.

"I thought I might go to Wisconsin. I haven't visited Mom or Dad in a long while. I kind of hoped to spend some time on the road. Maybe I could go up and over the Mackinac Bridge one way, and then go through or around Chicago the other time. Maybe I even could take one of the ferries across Lake Michigan, like the time I went with Dad."

"Hmm, that sounds like a very good idea. You could spend a little time with your mom's side of the family, even though they're all pretty much here now. That does sound like a good plan, and since you will be 18, you can make decisions for yourself, although Uncle Ron and I would still like to be kept in the mix, if you know what I mean."

"No problem, Grandma. I promise to text or call you every day."

Grandma smiled. "That's the most enthused I've seen you in a long time. I think a road trip on your bike is an excellent idea. I know how much you enjoy riding, just like your folks."

"I do like the freedom, Grandma. That's for sure. I only wish I would have ridden more with Mom and Dad when I was younger."

"Well," Grandma was waxing philosophic, "someday you could take your own children on rides."

Harley laughed, "That's a long way away, Grandma. A long, long way."

"One never knows, Harley. Just take it all day by day."

Harley grinned over at her. "Just be careful, Grandma, or I might just drag you along with me on that bike. Dad's trailer does hold two people, you know."

Grandma guffawed. "In your dreams, boy! You'll not get me on that monster of a machine for any length of time."

Harley laughed, "Well, maybe around the block then."

Grandma laughed too. "Deal."

They had reached the house. Harley pulled into the driveway, drove to a stop outside the garage, and shut down the car. He hopped out and ran around the other side to open the door for Grandma. "There's the gentleman I know and love," she cooed. She reached up and gave Harley a peck on the cheek. "I love you, young man. Don't you ever forget it."

Harley smiled down at her. "Never."

He slammed the door behind her, and then popped the trunk to retrieve some party items, while she headed for the door.

"Now, if only he never forgets how much that young lady loves him, then we'll be getting somewhere," she whispered to herself.

"Did you say something, Grandma?" Harley asked.

"No, just talking to myself. Making sure we're all ready for the party."

"I'm sure it will be fine, Grandma. You always know how to have a good time."

"That I do, Harley. That I do."

The party went off without a hitch. Harley enjoyed visiting with his relatives, received some nice gifts, including some Harley-Davidson accessories for his motorcycle, and was actually disappointed when it all came to an end.

Not everyone had to leave right away, so Harley gathered together some of his cousins, and they made plans to go to Cedar Point and ride the rollercoasters the next day. It was something he had been missing, something he had intended to do for the past couple of years, and now he was able to make good on it.

The next day, two carloads of teenagers and twenty-somethings headed over the Michigan border into Ohio for a day of fun in the sun in Sandusky. Harley loved riding the roller coasters almost as much as riding his motorcycle. Almost.

As the day turned to night, and the cousins headed back into Michigan, Harley settled back in the seat of his cousin's pickup and relived the day, the rides, the laughs, even the junk food. It had been a perfect day. Almost. Abby should have been there. Then it would have been perfect.

He shook his head. In a few days, he would be 18. He could do what he wanted. And what he wanted was to return to Plymouth. Alone. He was leaving nothing to chance. No one else would be harmed.

His plan was simple. He was going to Wisconsin. That much was true. He missed his mom and dad more than he ever cared to admit, and he had not visited their graves in a very long time. He felt as if he was neglecting them and their memory. He was going to spend a couple days with his grandma in Wisconsin, go back to his old hometown for a day or two, make the rounds, and then head through upper Michigan to Sault Ste. Marie. His parents had gotten him a passport, so he was going to take advantage of that and travel through Canada.

From the Soo Locks he would travel over to New York, taking in historic sites in the Northeast all along the way. Even if his ultimate plan was to return to Plymouth, he saw no reason to pass up the opportunity to do what his mother and father had done all along, which was take in the country's history. He had caught the history bug from his family, and he knew that for the remainder of his life studying American history would not be a chore, but a vocation.

Now, all he had to do was patiently wait for the calendar to reach his birthdate. He planned to leave the day after. Harley nestled his way deeper into the seat and closed his eyes. As he dozed, Plymouth waited, as did something he could never have imagined in his wildest dreams. Across the ocean, nearly 4000 miles away from where Harley snoozed, a volcano began to awaken.

Plymouth Rock

Fulfillment

"NOW, HARLEY, PLEASE promise me you'll be careful, and you will stay in touch with me," Grandma Schultz was saying as Harley donned his helmet and pulled the strap snugly under his chin.

"I will Grandma," he replied. "Don't worry, I will be fine."

"Call me when you stop for the day, or when you get to your other grandma's house."

"I will."

"Now give your grandma a hug and be on your way."

"I'll do you one better." Harley leaned down, pecked his grandma on the cheek, and then hugged her tightly. "I'll miss you most of all," he whispered.

"I'll miss you too. Have fun, and enjoy your time and newfound freedom," she smiled. "You're 18 now, and we will always be here for you, but now you need to live your life as you see fit. I pray that you will be happy and find fulfillment. I love you, Harley."

"I love you, too, Grandma. Thank you for all you've done for me. I really mean that. I don't know what I would have done if you hadn't let me stay with you."

"You're very welcome. Now go, before I change my mind and keep you here." She grinned at him, but Harley could see tears behind the smile.

"Okay, Grandma. See you later." Harley mounted his Road Glide, loaded and prepped for long distance riding, slid on his sunglasses, fired the engine, shifted the big machine into gear, released the clutch, and slowly pulled away from the place that had been his home for the last two years. His dad's mini camper now trailed Harley's own bike as he headed out of the driveway.

As he rounded the curve and rode out of sight, he was glad to have on those sunglasses. They hid the mist that had formed in his own eyes when he had caught that glimpse of sorrow in his grandmother's eyes. If she would have cried, he…well, he didn't want to think about. "Time to start my new life," he stated resolutely, barely hearing his voice over the rumble of the V-twin engine that was purring like a kitten, yet ready to roar as soon as Harley made it out on the open road.

"Fulfillment," Harley thought. "That's a great word, considering the circumstances." He wondered if that was positive or negative.

Harley had decided that his route would follow more state highways than interstates. He reasoned that he had not driven much with the trailer attached. He had just recently installed a hitch, and then he had taken the trailer for a 30 minute trial run. Other than that, he didn't have experience with it. Driving 70 miles per hour on I-94 with the trailer attached seemed a little daunting, whereas 55-60 on a two lane highway gave him a great deal of confidence.

With that decision made, he headed down to Monroe, where he picked up M-50 west. Just outside of the city, Harley spotted the fairgrounds and the turnoff to the community college. He had considered taking classes there before attending the University of Michigan, but he had received scholarships for all four years at U of M, so it made more sense just to start in Ann Arbor in the fall.

As he rumbled toward US-12, passing through Dundee and Tecumseh, he stretched his legs out on the highway pegs that extended away from his crash bars and lowers. Pushing a couple of buttons on the stereo system, he relaxed and hummed along with his road songs compilation from his iPod. He set the cruise control, leaned into his backrest, and smiled. Freedom of the road. The wind in his face. The unparalleled view from the seat of a motorcycle. His mom and dad had been right. This was the way to travel.

As if by divine intervention, or just wishful thinking, Kid Rock's *Born Free* began to play over the speakers. Harley sang along to the lyrics, completely enveloped in the song, the sights, the moment in time. He was completely at ease, with his entire future unwritten, his whole life ahead of him. "Fulfillment." Great word.

US-12 took Harley completely across the Lower Peninsula, finally running back into I-94 over near the small town of New Buffalo. He stopped there for a quick lunch and to fill up the bike with fuel. He jumped on the interstate, knowing the next couple of hours would be the most challenging for him. As he crossed into Indiana, he knew in an hour he would be riding alone, for the first time, in one of the largest cities in America-Chicago.

He had traveled this route many times with his parents, but he had always been a passenger, opting many times to snooze as his dad or mom fought the traffic. Now, it was his turn, and he was a little nervous.

He had done his homework, however, and he knew exactly what roads and even what lanes to be in as he weaved through the city. His dad had showed him the route that seemed to work well, and best of all, minus all the tollbooths that seemed to surround Chicago.

Once Harley made it through the Loop, the nickname for the downtown area, he continued on until the I-90/I-94 split. He continued on I-94 until he reached Highway 41, which would take him through Waukegan, and also take him near Great Lakes, the training base for new naval inductees. The highway rejoined I-94 right at the Illinois/Wisconsin border.

Harley was feeling ecstatic as he crossed into Wisconsin. He decided to pull off at the Kenosha exit for gas, knowing that a White Castle restaurant was there. He enjoyed the "gut bombs" or "sliders" as they had been christened. After topping off the tank, he stopped and grabbed four of the tasty little hamburgers that he often craved. In the Detroit area, there were plenty of these burger joints, but in Wisconsin this one was about it.

"Might be a while before I get another, so I guess I should enjoy it," he murmured as he placed his order.

After his snack, it was only about an hour or so until he'd make his grandmother's house. Harley had to grin, remembering his threat to his father to tattle to Grandma if Harley had not been allowed to accompany him on the trip to Roanoke. His dad had caved almost immediately, knowing that his wife's mother was nearly as tough, and sometimes as difficult, as his own mother in Michigan. Harley had played his cards correctly that day.

Harley finally reached his grandmother's house, and as he pulled in, a number of cousins came pouring out of the house. Apparently Michigan Grandma had informed Wisconsin Grandma of his approximate arrival time, so she had a welcoming party waiting.

A party it was. Even though he had such a great party in Michigan, Grandma Cannon, Harley's mom's maiden name, had prepared a cookout, with Harley as the guest of honor. His aunts, uncles, and cousins from his mom's side all wanted to check out his ride. Many asked if he could open the trailer and show them how it became a camper. A couple of them even crawled inside to test it out.

All in all, it was a great evening, with a beautiful sunset and cool, comfortable temperatures. A campfire was in order, and soon everyone was gathered around the flames, roasting marshmallows and making s'mores. Harley kicked back in a lounge chair and took in the ambience.

"So now that you're all filled up, Harley, what kind of plans do you have for your time in Wisconsin?" Grandma asked.

Harley replied, "I thought I would maybe take in a baseball game at Miller Park and maybe go downtown to the Harley-Davidson Museum. I'll probably spend a couple of days here, and then I want to go visit Mom and Dad, and spend a couple of days there."

"That sounds like a good plan. I'm sure some of your relatives would be glad to accompany you to the game or the museum." A chorus of assents was heard from around the fire.

"Great!" Harley smiled. "I think the Brewers are home tomorrow night, so why don't we do the game first, and then do the museum trip the following day?"

It worked out perfectly, and Harley spent the next two days enjoying his stay in southeastern Wisconsin. Deep down, though, he was beginning to get the itch to return to his home of 16 years, and to visit his mom and dad's graves. It had been a long time.

The morning after touring the museum, Harley once again loaded up his bike, double-checked the trailer, and gave his grandma a hug. "Thanks for letting me stay here, Grandma. I had a great time."

"You are welcome here any time, Harley. You know that. I hope you can make it over here often. I know you're going to be busy going to school and all, but we don't want you to forget where your roots are. Please come and see us whenever you can."

Harley gazed at his grandma, searching her eyes for a deeper meaning, and the realization that she was missing her daughter, Harley's mom, was evident.

"I miss her too, Grandma. Every day."

Grandma shook her head and tears appeared. "Your mom was such a wonderful woman, Harley. I still can't believe she's gone, even after all these years."

Harley didn't know what to say, so he simply pulled his grandma close to him and whispered, "I'll tell her hello from you when I make it back home later today."

Grandma pulled back and smiled up at him. "You do that, Harley." She wiped the tears from her eyes. "You do that," she repeated, "and tell your dad hello from us too."

Harley smiled back at his grandma, "I will, Grandma. Thank you again for everything."

One more hug, and once again Harley mounted his machine, strapped on his helmet, slid on the sunglasses, and fired the engine.

With a wave to his grandma, he pulled away and headed west, back to where he had been born and raised, back to the formative years of his life, back to old friends, and back to visit his mom's and dad's burial site.

As the bike rumbled beneath him, Harley took a deep breath and sighed. The fun part of the trip was over. He was unsure how his family's old friends would react when he showed up again. He took a deep breath and sighed. His priority was to visit the cemetery, do any necessary landscaping, and leave something behind as a memorial. Whatever occurred beyond that would be simply paying a visit to the old hometown to do some reminiscing.

The two hour ride was uneventful, and as he pulled into town, he decided to gas up first, and then he would start making the rounds. Sure enough, the first stop resulted in running into a couple of his old classmates that were working at the gas station. They seemed happy to see him, and he spent 15 minutes just recalling good times in school.

Harley asked about some of his old teachers, and it sounded as if a number of them were at the high school teaching summer courses. He decided he would make that his next stop, and with handshakes and a wave, he was off again.

It was only a couple of miles to the high school, and as he pulled in, he noted that the parking lot was full of automobiles, some of which he recognized as his old teachers' cars.

Harley stopped the bike at the back of the lot, where he would be able to easily maneuver the bike and trailer out of the parking area later on. He strolled inside the building where he had spent his first two years of high school, and proceeded to the office to see who might be available.

The secretary, Mrs. Adams, who had been good friends with Harley's mom, recognized Harley at once. She rushed over and gave him a big hug. "Harley, it's so great to see you! How are you? What brings you here?"

"Hi, Mrs. Adams, it's great to see you too. I just decided to make a trip here and visit Mom and Dad."

Mrs. Adams nodded understandingly. "We all miss your mom and dad, Harley. They were wonderful people, and they did so much for the community." She paused for a moment, and then she continued, "Do you have any other plans?"

"I thought I could maybe stop by some of the rooms and see some of my old teachers. Would that be okay?"

"That would be fine, Harley. I'm sure they would be happy to see you. If you need anything while you're in town, please feel free to stop over. You know where we live."

"Thanks, Mrs. Adams. I probably will just camp out at the park, but I do appreciate your offer. Please tell Mr. Adams hello from me."

"I'll do that, Harley. Thank you for stopping by. Take care of yourself."

"Bye, Mrs. Adams."

Harley exited the office and headed through the commons and into the gym, where he looked around and fondly remembered the days of gym class and nights of basketball practices and games against rival schools. His spirits were very high. Everyone he had seen thus far had treated him as if he had never been gone, and it was obvious that his mom and dad had been well respected. They had made a positive impact in this small town, and their contributions would not be soon forgotten.

Harley continued his tour, occasionally stopping in a classroom and visiting with former teachers. Every single one of them expressed their joy at seeing him again, asked what his college plans were, and shared stories about his parents. By the end of the visit, Harley was entirely convinced that his decision to return had been the correct choice.

With a quick stop at the office to once again say goodbye to Mrs. Adams, Harley decided that he would also make a quick stop at the elementary/middle school and see who might be there.

The first person he saw was his favorite custodian, Mr. Cooper. Harley had known him from the time he had started kindergarten all the way through 8th grade. Mr. Cooper also owned a Harley-Davidson, and he and his wife had often ridden with Harley's parents around Wisconsin on overnighters or just long Sunday rides to the Mississippi River through the driftless area of southwestern Wisconsin.

Mr. Cooper grasped Harley's hand and yanked him into a bear hug, nearly smothering him. "Harley Schultz, are you a sight for sore eyes? How are you? What have you been up to?"

Harley grinned, "Hey, Mr. Cooper, I'm doing well, thank you. I decided to come up and visit my old stomping grounds." Harley paused for a second. "Mostly I just wanted to come and see Mom and Dad."

Mr. Cooper nodded sadly. "I sure do miss your folks, Harley. We always had so much fun together. The missus and I visit the cemetery often. We kind of took it upon ourselves to care and maintain for their graves. Hope you don't mind."

Harley was speechless. He had no idea that anyone would have done such a thing. Finally he was able to continue the conversation. "Wow, Mr. Cooper, I had no idea! Thank you so much!"

"It's my honor, Harley. Your mom and dad did a lot for our family over the years, and it's a small way of thanking them. Matter of fact, I was just out there yesterday, mowing and trimming."

"That makes it easy on me," Harley replied. "I was wondering how I would manage, seeing as I am on my bike and all."

"You are?" Mr. Cooper asked. "Well, let's go take a look at your baby."

They strolled back out to the parking lot, and Mr. Cooper whistled as he approached the Road Glide. "Nice bike, and I see you have your dad's trailer. How do you like riding with that attached?"

"Not too bad. Hardly know that it's back there. I'm going to eventually set up camp out at the park by the lake after I leave here. Have to stop and grab a few supplies, and then I think I'll just sit around a campfire and watch the sunset."

"That sounds like a great plan. Tell you what, I'll let you continue your visit, I'll call Mrs. Cooper, and we are going to treat you to dinner. We have our camper all set up out there for the summer. We are parked at #84, right on the corner of the lake. Know where I mean?"

Harley nodded, and Mr. Cooper continued, "Have dinner with us around the campfire, please. I know Mrs. Cooper would love to see you."

Harley could hardly refuse. "What time?"

"Let's say 7:00, and don't you bring a thing. It is our treat."

"Okay," Harley laughed, "I'm looking forward to it."

"Great! Now go on in there. A couple of your mom and dad's friends are in their classrooms. I'm sure they would be glad to see you as well. I need to make that phone call."

"Thanks, Mr. Cooper. If I don't see you before I head over to the campground, I'll see you at 7."

"Okay, now go," he said, trying to sound gruff. "I have work to do."

Harley grinned, and headed back inside. He spent the next hour and a half visiting with more of his former teachers, as well as family friends. Many fond memories resurfaced, and Harley was feeling more and more content about his homecoming. Finally, he said his goodbyes, drove over to the grocery store, grabbed some supplies for the campground, ran into more people he knew, and eventually escaped back outside.

It was only a few minutes out to the lake. Harley stopped in the office, paid for a site, and quickly drove over to the site. He deftly unhooked the trailer from his motorcycle, and in a matter of minutes he had the camper set up for the night. Looking around, he was pleased to see that some extra firewood had been left behind at the site, so he didn't even need to purchase any right away. He decided to take a walk along the shore for a little while, and then he could head over to the Cooper's campsite.

Harley walked along the beach, watching some young children build sand castles, while others romped in the shallows. Once he was beyond them, he began searching the shore for flat rocks. One of his favorite past times growing up was skipping stones, and he had become quite adept at it.

Skipping stones brought back memories of Anna and the short time they had spent together along the ocean shore. Then his thoughts turned to her cousin Abby, and the many good times they had spent together. Both of the girls' faces were embedded into his psyche, and it was all Harley could do to not cave in to his desire to reunite with Abby.

"I can't," he said aloud. "I can't have her be in danger because of me," he resolutely finished. He shook away those thoughts, and the grumbling in his stomach reminded him that he should probably head over to the Cooper's campsite.

Being quite familiar with the campground layout, he found site 84 easily, and as he approached he noted Mrs. Cooper walking around the campfire, watching some meat cook on a grill that had been lowered over the fire from a tripod that stood sentinel over the burning coals.

"Harley!" Mrs. Cooper cried when she noticed Harley's approach. "It's so good to see you!" She rushed over and threw her arms around him.

Harley picked her up and swung her around, both of them laughing. It was good to be in the company of close friends again. It had been a long time. The Coopers were as close to family as Harley had in his old hometown. That was a fact. They had always been there for the Schultz family through thick and thin. Harley fondly recalled campfires, garage parties, and just long talks with both of them.

The Cooper children were older than Harley, although he had known them growing up. Now all three of them were married and gone, leaving the parents as empty nesters. Both had adopted Harley as a surrogate child, always welcome in their home, as well as in their hearts. It was for that reason Harley had accepted their invitation. No one outside of his family, and maybe Abby, knew him that well.

Harley set Mrs. Cooper back down. She turned and yelled into the camper, "Mr. Cooper, Harley is here." The Coopers liked to call each other Mr. and Mrs., as opposed to their given names, a trait that Harley found both amusing and endearing.

Mr. Cooper appeared at the door of the camper, a huge grin on his face. "Come on over by the fire, Harley. Have a seat. Dinner is just about ready. Hope you're hungry."

"Actually, I am," Harley replied. "It smells really good."

"Mrs. Cooper is a great cook. We decided to throw some steaks and baked potatoes on the fire. Sound good?"

"Sounds great!" Harley exclaimed. "You guys shouldn't have gone to all this trouble though."

"No trouble," Mrs. Cooper responded, "we had already planned on a cookout. What's one more piece of meat and another potato or two? Now grab a plate, help yourself to whatever fixings you want, and dig in."

Harley didn't have to be told twice. Besides the meat and potatoes, Mrs. Cooper had a fruit salad and coleslaw, along with a cooler full of assorted beverages. Harley loaded up his plate, and then sat down in the all too familiar chair-in-a-bag that so many campers used.

"So tell us, what else is new?" Mr. Cooper said, as he sat down beside Harley.

"Let him eat," Mrs. Cooper protested. "The boy is all skin and bones."

"Trust me, that's not skin and bones," Mr. Cooper disagreed. "You've really filled out, Harley. I'm not sure I could take you anymore in a wrestling match. I remember picking you up and tossing you around like a sack of potatoes. Not sure I could do that now."

Harley laughed, fondly recalling how Mr. Cooper, and for that matter, even Mrs. Cooper, used to grapple with him. Mrs. Cooper was extremely strong, and just to prove it, she would sometimes grab Harley, throw him over her shoulder, and stroll around the Cooper yard, with Harley helpless to do anything but beg to be set down.

While it would normally have been embarrassing for a teenage boy to be flung about by a woman, Mrs. Cooper was no ordinary woman. Harley had never once fought the urge to fight back. He just let Mrs. Cooper have her way, and once she was done, she would unceremoniously plop him on the ground, his face beet red, but laughing all the same. She was like another mom to him. Mr. Cooper was like a second dad.

Those thoughts made it easy to start a conversation that continued throughout dinner, recalling all the old times, the weekend rides, everything a boy growing up in the Midwest could enjoy. Harley realized that he had grown up never wanting for anything, and that for the most part, his life had been a simple one. He had also been given all the love and nurturing that a family, and in this case, two families could give. It was like a wolf pack, everyone looking out for the others. Harley could not have felt more secure at this moment.

They finished their dinner and settled in around the campfire as the sun began to set over the lake. A slight breeze brought the temperature down a few degrees, leaving a very comfortable climate around the campground. An orange moon rising in the east cast a Halloween like appearance through the trees.

It was in this setting that Mr. Cooper asked, "So what are your plans for the remainder of your visit?"

Harley leaned back into his chair and replied, "I'll probably go over to the cemetery tomorrow morning. I have a couple of mementos I want to leave there. I had figured on cleaning up around the graves, but I guess I won't have to do that because you have already done that for me. By the way, Mrs. Cooper, thank you for doing that for Mom and Dad. I'm sure they appreciate it."

"It's our pleasure, Harley," Mrs. Cooper answered.

"After that, I might drive by the old house and see what it looks like. Then maybe I'll hit the state park and climb the mound. I always liked doing that and checking out the view."

"That sounds like fun. I haven't been up there in a while myself. Maybe Mrs. Cooper and I will have to do that one of these days." Mr. Cooper commented.

Mrs. Cooper responded, "That does sound like fun. Maybe this coming weekend, Mr. Cooper?"

Her husband nodded, then returned the conversation to Harley. "Anything else?"

Harley was unsure if he should say anything about his plan, but since he was now officially on his own, he decided it wouldn't matter much if he shared his future adventures.

"I think the following day I'm going to head for the U.P., and maybe stop at Mackinac, cross the bridge, and maybe go out to the island."

"That sounds like fun," Mrs. Cooper put in. "I remember how much fun we had with your parents when we went there."

Mr. Cooper asked, "Then from there, you'll head back to your grandmother's?"

Harley hesitated, and then he shook his head. "No, I'm going to go up to the Soo Locks. From there I'm going up into Canada."

"Doing a Circle Lake tour?" Mr. Cooper asked, although by the tone in his voice, Harley knew that Mr. Cooper already suspected something else.

"No, I'm going to head east toward New England. Cross over in upstate New York, and check out places like Lake Placid, Fort Ticonderoga, and Saratoga. There are a lot of historical places that

I would like to visit. Kind of want to continue doing what my mom and dad did. You know, they were always the history buffs."

"Well, that sounds like fun," Mrs. Cooper commented.

"Then home from there?" Mr. Cooper pressed Harley, knowing full well what the answer would be.

Harley stared at Mr. Cooper and the shook his head. "No, I'm going to go through Vermont, New Hampshire, Maine…and Massachusetts," he finished quietly.

"Harley, no," Mrs. Cooper cried out. "You're not really going back there, are you?"

Harley had heard Mrs. Cooper, but he had continued to stare at Mr. Cooper, directing his answer more at him than her. "I want to see Boston, Lexington, Concord. All of that Revolutionary War stuff." He continued to gaze at Mr. Cooper.

"And Plymouth," Mr. Cooper stated matter-of-factly.

"And Plymouth."

There was a long silence. Mr. Cooper lowered his gaze, grabbed a poker, and stirred the coals in the fire, before adding another log onto the top of the small blaze. The fire slowly began to grow again.

Finally, Mr. Cooper spoke, "I'm in no position to tell you what to do, Harley, but may I ask why you are going back there?"

"I just have to," Harley replied.

Mr. Cooper continued to poke at the fire. Then he looked over at his wife, who appeared frightened by Harley's travel plans. She nodded at her husband, and he returned his gaze to Harley.

Mr. Cooper took a deep breath. "Harley, I know your parents were God fearing people. They took you to church, raised you in a Christian manner, taught you morals and ethics, and you have turned out to be a fine young man. But, and this is a big but, do you feel it is wise to continue this…quest?"

"Probably not wise, but I'm going just the same."

Mr. Cooper sighed. "Harley, you believe in God, right?"

Harley nodded.

"Then I'm assuming you believe in Satan, and evil?"

Harley nodded again.

Mr. Cooper paused for a moment, whether for dramatic effect or because he was considering what to say next, Harley didn't know.

"Harley, I believe," he looked at his wife, "we believe, that this endeavor of yours can bring no good. When your mother died, we believed it was an accident. The following year, when your dad nearly died, and your friend and her mother did, we began to wonder at the wisdom of your search. When your father died the following year, we assumed this would be over. Then you went to Plymouth last year, and another friend of yours died in a freak accident. If that is what it was."

Harley was on the defensive. "Do you think I haven't thought of that?"

Mr. Cooper replied, "I can see by your demeanor that you obviously have. So, I ask you, is it worth it?"

"I promised my mom," Harley said simply.

"Promised her what? To get yourself killed? No, Harley, this is an evil endeavor. No good can come from it. It makes me wonder about that young lady you were seeing, Abby, is it?"

"What about her? And what do you know about it?"

"I keep in touch with both of your grandmothers, as well as your uncle. They filled me in. Your grandma in Michigan told me you broke off your relationship with Abby right after your friend Chris was killed. Now I'm no genius, but it seems to me that you did that to keep her out of the line of fire, so to speak. I think you know, deep down, that this is a bad idea. How am I doing?"

Harley didn't say anything for a moment. Then he cried out, "Everyone who was involved in this search for Atlantis has died, and they have all been violent, awful deaths. I couldn't let that happen to her too!"

"You're in love with her, aren't you?" Mrs. Cooper said quietly.

Harley spun his head around to face her. He couldn't answer, and she saw the hurt in his eyes and nodded. "I thought so."

"I won't allow whatever this is to harm her," Harley finally murmured. "If something happens to me, so be it, but I want to know the truth."

"Even if the truth is beyond human reasoning?" asked Mr. Cooper.

Harley didn't answer. Mr. Cooper continued, "Harley, your mother would not have wanted you to put yourself in such a perilous situation. She may have searched for Atlantis, but she never had any clue what horrible things would follow these discoveries. Please reconsider this. It's a fool's errand. No good can come from it."

Harley replied, "You're probably right, but I'm going just the same."

Mr. Cooper sighed, "What are you hoping to find? Roanoke and Jamestown provided you clues and amulets, if I've been reading the papers correctly. What led you to Plymouth anyway?"

Harley remained silent, but Mr. Cooper read right through the silence. "You do have another clue, don't you?" he exclaimed.

Harley nodded. "My dad had made a list of people, and he was killed before he could explain it to me. I deciphered some of it, and it led us to Plymouth, but Chris was killed before we discovered anything."

"So you have nothing more to go on?"

Harley didn't answer. Mr. Cooper read his appearance. He nodded, "You found something else, didn't you? Something you haven't shared with anyone. Not the police, not your family, not Abby. Am I right?"

Harley didn't answer, and Mr. Cooper realized he had hit upon a truth. "Well, whatever it is, obviously it is important, and you are bound and determined to decipher it all. Okay, you need not share anything with us, Harley, but please know that both of us love you as if you were one of our own. We don't want you to go, and we believe that this Atlantis search is cursed in some way. It has evil written all over it. All we can do is ask God to bless you and protect you from whatever lies in wait for you."

Harley found his voice. "Thank you, Mr. and Mrs. Cooper. I do appreciate all you have done, and maybe I am a fool for continuing, but I made a promise to my mother at her grave that I would see this through, and that's what I am going to do. Dad was pursuing this right up until his death, and he left me some clues. I just wish he could have explained it all to me. It just seems like I'm missing something. Whatever it is, I'm betting I will find it in Plymouth. It's like I am predestined to be involved. Events only occur when I am there, so the only way to finish this is to go."

Mr. and Mrs. Cooper looked at each other blankly. They had tried to reason with the young man, but to no avail. He was going, come hell or high water. Unfortunately, that adage would be more prophetic than either adult could imagine.

Harley decided to call it a day. He thanked the Coopers for their hospitality, giving them both a long hug. "Please be careful, Harley," Mrs. Cooper whispered.

"I will," Harley promised.

Mr. Cooper was not as tactful. "I don't want to attend another funeral, Harley. I hope somehow you will reconsider, but if not, I pray the Lord's blessings to you. Please be careful," he echoed Mrs. Cooper's sentiments. "Stay in touch with us. We miss you around here."

"I will," Harley said, "and please tell your kids I said hello. I really had a great time growing up here and spending time with your family. You two really are the best. I couldn't have asked for a better childhood. Thank you for being such a big part of it."

With that, Harley turned away from the friendly campfire, and returned to his own site. He decided against a fire, and instead readied himself for bed. Sleep would not come easy, as he tossed and turned in the little trailer. To make matters worse, a thunderstorm whipped up, dousing the campground for the better part of an hour. As he rolled over for what seemed the hundredth time, he knew tomorrow would be a long day. Finally he nodded off in a tumultuous sleep, filled with thoughts of his mother and father, the Coopers, Anna and her parents, and finally Abby.

— ((•)) —

Harley awoke early the next morning, headed to the showers, cleaned himself up, and returned to his campsite. He had made the decision to leave for New England this very day, stopping long enough to visit the cemetery.

By 7 a.m. he was packed, the trailer attached, and the campsite cleaned up. He stopped at the office long enough to check out, and then he headed for the cemetery. Once he reached the graveyard, he pulled in, heading to his parents' site. When he pulled up in front of the headstone, he shut down the motorcycle and dismounted.

Silence greeted Harley. No one else was in sight. He had the entire cemetery to himself. He reached inside the touring pack and pulled out a small bag. After closing and latching the pack, he walked slowly to the graves.

When he reached the headstone, he knelt down and whispered aloud, "Hi, Mom. Hi, Dad. It's been a long time. I've wanted to stop and see you for a long time. The Coopers have been doing a nice job keeping the place looking nice. They are really good friends, so much so that they tried talking me out of returning. I wonder if they aren't right about this whole thing."

Harley reached into the bag and pulled out two gold-colored pieces, one in the shape of a hurricane and the other in the shape of tornado. "It didn't seem that flowers would be the right thing to leave, especially considering the situation, so Mom," Harley gently placed the hurricane amulet beneath her name, "this is for you, and Dad, this is for you." He set the tornado amulet under his father's name.

"Some people would see this as morbid, but I don't. To me, it represents all that we've been through, and I am going to persevere until I find the truth. If the Coopers are right, and this whole pursuit is doomed or evil, then I will just pray that God will protect me."

With that Harley bowed his head and prayed that he would be guided and protected from any evil, that the good Lord would bless his family and friends, and that he himself might act in a manner befitting of his family. After an "Amen," Harley rose, stood over the graves, and spoke one last sentence. "I love you, Mom and Dad. I hope I can make you proud."

He turned to go. Reaching his bike, he peered at the trailer. One of the tires was flat, a nail sticking out of it. Harley looked up at the sky, which was beginning to darken. "That's not the answer I was looking for."

Harley replaced the flat tire with the spare, stopped by the local garage to have the damaged tire patched, and then headed over to the school. He wanted to say goodbye to Mr. Cooper.

Mr. Cooper heard the motorcycle rumbling into the lot and was waiting for Harley once he pulled up and dismounted. "Looks like you've decided to head out a little early."

"Yeah, I stopped by the cemetery already. I just wanted to come and say goodbye to you. Thank you for last night, I really appreciate everything you've done. Please tell Mrs. Cooper goodbye from me as well."

"I'll do that. Take care of yourself, Son. We really enjoyed our visit. Don't be a stranger."

"Thanks, Mr. Cooper. I'll try. I mean it."

Mr. Cooper nodded, "Good luck, Harley, and God bless you."

They embraced each other, and Harley climbed back aboard his bike. Once he fired the engine, he waved one last time at Mr. Cooper, and then pulled away.

Harley headed northwest and picked up Highway 22 near Wild Rose. He was going to follow that up toward Oconto, where he could pick up 41and ride through Peshtigo and Marinette. He would cross the Wisconsin/Michigan border there, and then pick up 35, a two lane highway built right along the Lake Michigan shoreline. Harley had some great views of the lake and dunes as he made his way to Escanaba.

It was midafternoon when he stopped there for a late lunch and to fill up his tank. It was still almost 150 miles to the Straits of Mackinac, and Harley decided he could still make it before dark, and since he had the trailer, he didn't need a motel reservation, just a tent site at a Triple C. There were campgrounds on either side of the bridge, and depending upon what was available on the north side of the bridge, he would take whatever was first available.

He reached St. Ignace and pulled off at an overlook to stare at the magnificent Mackinac Bridge, one of the longest suspension bridges in the world. Harley had traversed it a number of times in his 18 years, and he always marveled at its construction, size, and beauty.

He decided to cross over for the night, and then cross back in the morning and head for Sault Ste. Marie and the Canadian border. He mounted his bike, and drove the short distance to the on ramp that led onto I-75. He stopped at the tool booth, paid the fee, and pulled slowly onto the bridge. The weather had held. He had stayed ahead of the storm, but as he peered to the west, he could see the storm clouds gathering. It would be another stormy night.

Harley stayed in the right lane, which was made of concrete, but he could not resist peeking at the left lane, which was made of metal gratings that enabled him to look through and see the water hundreds of feet below. The thrill never lessened when he crossed the Mighty

Mac. It was an incredible feat of engineering, meant to be a useful passage from the Lower Peninsula to the Upper, but to many, Harley included, it was one of the greatest tourist attractions around.

Once across the five mile bridge, he pulled off at the first exit, which had a sign inviting travelers to the Triple C Campground. He reached the campground in a matter of minutes, stopped in the lodge to reserve a site, and then drove over and set up. Just in the nick of time, he was able to open the trailer and duck inside. The storms had finally caught up with him, and for the next couple of hours he listened to the sounds of thunder and watched the lightning streak across the sky.

Harley actually felt content in his surroundings, so much so that the storm actually enabled him to doze off. His restless night before, accompanied by his emotional stop at the graveyard, and his 400 mile jaunt, had worn him out. Soon, he was out cold. The storm passed, and Harley slept.

———◦《◊》◦———

The next morning Harley awoke refreshed and ready for action. He was hungry too, as he had last eaten the previous afternoon. Harley climbed out of the trailer, which was none the worse for wear after the storm. Digging through his cooler, he found some fruit, small containers of milk and Tupperware bowls with cereal sealed inside. He didn't even bother to take time to sit down. Instead he ate while he leaned against the trailer. Quickly cleaning up his dishes, as well as cleaning himself up in the shower room, Harley was ready to go before most of the campers were up and about. "Hope I don't wake up everyone when I fire up my baby. Oh well, they can sleep when they're dead."

The engine on the Road Glide rumbled to life, Harley popped the shifter into first, released the clutch, and pulled out of the campground, retracing his route back to the highway and back over the bridge. It was a glorious morning, and Harley was in high spirits as he looked out at Mackinac Island, situated in the middle of the lake. He could just make out two large, white buildings. One, he knew, was the Grand Hotel, and the other was Fort Mackinac. He had toured both of them when he was younger, as well as the entire island.

He grinned at the thought of how the island was operated. No motor vehicles were allowed, and the basic modes of transportation were horse and buggy or bicycle. How Harley longed to take his Road Glide around the island, just once. That was a pipe dream, however. Not even the President of the United States could do that.

Once over the bridge, he continued up I-75 for about an hour, at which point he pulled off at the exit that would leave him near the Soo Locks. He wanted to see if a freighter might be passing through the locks. Much to his delight, and good fortune, a freighter was passing through. Not just any freighter either, but a very famous one.

Growing up near the Great Lakes, Harley was well aware of the ill-fated trip of the *Edmund Fitzgerald*, a 729 foot freighter that had sunk on November 10, 1975. The shipwreck had been immortalized in the song written by Gordon Lightfoot entitled *The Wreck of the Edmund Fitzgerald*. What few people knew was that another freighter, the *Arthur M. Anderson*, had been following behind the stricken freighter when it had disappeared beneath the monster waves that Lake Superior was notorious for whipping up in the late fall.

As Harley climbed the steps to the lookout area, there was the *Arthur M. Anderson*, plain as day, directly in front of him, barely an arm's length from him, as it rose higher and higher in the locks. It was a sight to behold, and Harley rejoiced in the fact that he had been at the right place at the right time to see a piece of history.

Noting that piece of history, and the sad fact that 29 men had perished during that stormy night, gave Harley a little perspective. Bad news made headlines. Seldom was good news highlighted by the media. Thinking of how many good people he knew, and how many good things they had done, Harley was a little disgusted that those acts of kindness were almost always overlooked, except for the people directly involved.

He shook his head, acknowledging that in his country, the United States, there was freedom of the press, which allowed the media to cover just about any event it wanted. Unfortunately, it seemed to Harley that the press would happily deliver nothing but bad news and discord if at all possible. As much as he appreciated his freedom, Harley sometimes wondered if it wasn't all a bit too much. People found loopholes, and most of the time it was greed, not truth, that drove them.

In Harley's case, he was not in search of riches or fame. He simply wanted to know the truth, and he wanted his mother's life and research to matter. Still, he struggled with the fact that so many people had already died. It was a catch-22, a double edged sword. The more he had pursued the truth, the more it had cost him.

Finally, the *Arthur M. Anderson* had made it through the locks and continued on its way. Harley climbed back down the stairs, returned to his motorcycle, and headed back to the highway and over the bridge that would lead him into another country-Canada.

After showing his passport to the young woman at the booth and stating his business, he was allowed entrance into the country to the north of his beloved America. Here, Harley knew, he was no longer under American law, so he knew he had to be careful. Ignorance of the law was no excuse, so he was keenly aware that he needed to be ever watchful as he rode along the Canadian highways.

For one thing, every sign for speed and distance was in kilometers instead of miles, so he was continuously calculating speed, distance and time. He reached Sudbury, Ontario, known for its nickel mining, around noon. Stopping for lunch and gasoline, he decided to see how far he could go. He was following Highway 17, and made it as far as Renfrew, when he decided to call it a day.

Harley was not far from Ottawa, and he had planned to turn off and head back into the U.S. near the town of Ogdensburg, New York. That would be a 100 mile trip first thing in the morning, and then he would head over to Plattsburgh, which was situated on Lake Champlain, the border between Vermont and New York.

The following morning he made that trip, and once he was back in the U.S., after being asked numerous questions at the border, he arrived in Plattsburgh. Now he had a choice to make. He could cross over Lake Champlain by ferry or head south to Fort Ticonderoga. He chose the latter, wanting to take in the big fort that had been a strategic defensive position in both the French and Indian War and the American Revolution.

Since he had gotten another early start, he made it to Fort Ticonderoga by early afternoon. He purchased a ticket, and spent the next couple of hours examining the cannons, guns, and barracks where American, British, and French soldiers had fought and died. Harley stared up at Mt. Defiance, across the river, and recalled how the British, led by General Burgoyne, had scaled the backside of it one night in 1777, and in the morning had trained their cannons down on Fort Ticonderoga. The Americans had surrendered the fort without a shot. Not exactly the most awe inspiring battle ever fought in the revolution, but nevertheless, one of strategic importance.

As Harley reached a campground in the Ticonderoga area, he knew that the following day would lead him to Burgoyne's next target. It was just south of where Harley made camp, at a place called Saratoga. There the tables would be turned, and a man that had gone down in history as one of the worst traitors of all time, would actually lead the Americans to an improbable victory and, ultimately, the surrender of Burgoyne and his entire army.

Benedict Arnold, the very synonym for traitor, had led American troops to the victory that would be the turning point in the war. He had been wounded in the leg, and as Harley stood at the Saratoga National Battlefield the next morning, he stared at a monument of a boot, with no name ascribed to it, only a statement reading that the memorial stood in honor of the hero of Saratoga.

Because of Arnold's heroism, the French had joined the war on the American side, thus giving the Americans much needed supplies and men. Harley shook his head and wondered what would have Benedict Arnold have become had he not turned traitor in 1780. "If he had just waited one more year, he probably would have been as big a hero as George Washington. The war was basically over in October of 1781. What a shame!" Harley thought.

From Saratoga, Harley headed toward Bennington, Vermont, where another important American victory had occurred. Ironically, the city of Bennington was in Vermont, but the battlefield was just a mile or so outside of town to the east, which actually placed it in the state of New York.

Harley was quite surprised that he had not known this little tidbit of information. He was beginning to recognize why his parents enjoyed history so much. The textbooks simply did not give a student enough information. Only by traveling and experiencing had he found the truth.

"Same reason I'm heading for Plymouth," Harley thought. "I want to know the truth."

Harley had decided to stay in Bennington that night. As he set up camp and started a fire, his phone buzzed. It was his grandma. True to his word, he had contacted her on a daily basis, mostly by text, but when he had reached Mackinac, she had called him. The Coopers had, of course, contacted her, bless their hearts, and had told her of Harley's plan to return to the East Coast.

She had not been happy at all to hear of his plans, but with little that she could do to prevent his trip she simply asked that he keep her informed of his whereabouts. He had continued to send her messages, along with photos, of his stops at Ticonderoga, Saratoga, and Bennington.

So it was somewhat of a surprise when he realized that she was actually calling him. "Hi, Grandma, this is a surprise. What's up?"

"Harley, are you still in Bennington?"

"Yeah, why?"

"Are you planning to go to Plymouth tomorrow?"

"Actually, I was. It's only about three and a half or four hours over there."

"Harley, do not go!" Grandma commanded.

Even through the phone, Harley could sense some sort of dread in her voice. "What are you talking about Grandma?"

"Harley, haven't you been watching the news?"

"Actually, no, it's been kind of nice staying off the grid and just living day to day without all the worries and hassles."

"Then you don't know about the volcano."

"Volcano?" Harley laughed. "What the heck are you talking about, Grandma? There's no volcano on the East Coast."

"I didn't say there was, Harley. I'm talking about one across the Atlantic Ocean. It's all over the news. It's beginning to erupt, and if it does it could cause a tsunami that could hit the entire East Coast. They are saying it could be hundreds of feet high and all the major cities may need to be evacuated. Do you understand, Harley? Don't go to the ocean. It's too dangerous. Do you think it's a coincidence that once again you are heading there, and once again nature is preparing something horrible? Please tell me you are not going to go."

"Grandma," Harley said as comfortingly as he could, "has it actually occurred yet? Has the volcano actually erupted? Has this tsunami already started for America?"

"Well, no, not yet, Harley, but the scientists are saying it's just a matter of time."

Harley was not convinced. "Grandma, scientists predict a lot of things, and half the time they can't even get the weather right, let alone predicting earthquakes and volcanoes. Even if a volcano erupts, that doesn't mean there will be a tsunami. That's from underwater earthquakes."

"This is different, Harley. It's called a mega tsunami, and it's not the result of any earthquake. It's due to a massive landslide. The scientists say part of the island would slide into the sea, causing a tsunami unlike any ever seen before."

"Okay, Grandma, let me look into it. If it seems that dangerous, I won't go, okay?"

If Grandma Schultz could have seen his face, she would have known better, but since she was only on her phone, she had to take Harley at his word. "Okay, Harley, thank you for listening. It looks like your trip has been quite educational to say the least."

"Oh yeah, Grandma, it's been really an eye opener. The more I do this, the more I understand why Mom and Dad were so into it. I can't believe all the stuff I've learned."

Harley could almost see Grandma's smile through the phone. "You are your parents' child. I'm glad you are enjoying yourself, but please keep an eye on the news. If the scientists are correct, people would have only hours to get away. You don't want to be caught in that mess. Understand?

"Got it, Grandma, I am going to see what this is all about as soon as we hang up. I'll check the internet on my phone."

Harley could hear Grandma's audible sigh of relief. "Thank you, Harley. I love you."

"Love you too, Grandma. I'll keep letting you know what I'm doing."

Harley hit the off button and immediately began searching the internet about the volcano. He found mixed information. First he found that there had been some research done on the island of La Palma, which was in the Canary Islands. There was a volcano that could erupt, and if it did, a landslide could occur, which could cause a tsunami.

Other websites debunked the possibility and said the science done was inaccurate and all of this was basically a media stunt to cause panic and cause a sensation. However, even these websites said that La Palma could erupt, but the possibility of a tsunami, mega or otherwise, was negligible.

Harley was on the horns of a dilemma. The most recent news did in fact state that there was volcanic activity in the Canary Islands. In the past there had been landslides as well. All of the pieces were there, but Harley was swayed more by the science against the possibility of a tsunami than for it.

In the back of his mind, however, one piece of history continued to pound in his skull. Atlantis, according to Plato, had experienced one day and night of earthquakes. The following day Atlantis had been swept from the earth by some sort of cataclysmic wave or flood.

Another thought entered his mind. He had long given up on coincidences, looking at events as connections instead. The connection he made now was that Columbus, along with many of the other explorers who came to America, stopped in the Canary Islands before heading out into the open ocean. Everything that Harley and his parents had studied about Atlantis began with the early European explorations. This was a sign to Harley that once again the Canary Islands were somehow going to play an integral role in the solution to this mystery.

With the news that there was indeed volcanic activity, which was being verified by scientists and media around the world, Harley could not shake the feeling of impending doom. Still, he had made a vow to his mother that he discover the truth about Atlantis one way or another, so he decided that he would travel to Plymouth in the morning. He would explore and investigate as much as he could, and if the worst case scenario was true, he would high tail it out of there just as fast as he could get his motorcycle to go.

He slept fitfully that night, and was up at the crack of dawn. He cleaned up, hooked the trailer to the bike, and was off before 7:00. He reached the Triple C where he had stayed the previous year. It wasn't noon yet, so he set up camp, and decided he would return to downtown Plymouth and grab a bite to eat.

After a quick lunch, he walked back down to the shoreline, studying the landscape and wondering how he would find the clue that had been in Stephen Hopkins' letter. He had made a copy of the note, not wanting to damage the original by continuously taking it out of a sealed bag. He studied it again.

> *Thus trusting in the Lord that*
> *the true meaneing of said discoveries may*
> *one day be revealed, the final talisman has thus beene*
> *bequeathed to the sea, being a strange and wonderfull*
> *occurrence whereas the sea itself has fallen away and the land*
> *exposed such a bolder that wouldst keep the secret secure*
> *until such time as wee may discover said truths.*
> *May the Lord direct you herein to eternity.*
>
> *Stephen Hopkins*

Harley traced his finger over the edge of the note, starting at the word *May* near the bottom left and following the words around until he reached the word *eternity*. He traced it again, and then again. The more he repeated the process, the more his mind began to picture an image. A wave. A huge wave. A tsunami. Harley gulped. Could he have really figured it out? Was Hopkins hinting that this shape was the key?

Immediately Harley's thoughts jumped from the note to the missing talisman. If somehow he managed to locate the talisman, would the shape be a wave? Then another thought entered his head. He pulled out copies of the other two amulets, the hurricane and the tornado, and set one next to the other.

He moved the two around, and noticed that they did fit together much like a jigsaw puzzle. He tried to imagine a wave-shaped amulet about the same size as the other two. He could see that if one was drawn to scale, it could possibly meet at the apex of the tornado, basically making the three amulets into one large amulet, a completed puzzle.

Studying the copies, he attempted to lay them together in the same manner as before, but this time with the two backsides of the amulets facing up. For the first time he saw what appeared to be pieces of a map. The nine pieces in the hurricane reminded Harley of islands, and the backside of the tornado had the appearance of both landmasses and water.

Harley breathed deeply. There was not enough information on the two pieces to make sense of it all, but now that Harley had found that they did seem to fit together, he was compelled to find the third piece. There had to be a way to find that boulder that Hopkins had mentioned. But how?

If it was underwater, how would he find it? Plus 400 years had gone by, so the bay had probably changed somewhat by human interaction. He stared out at the water, baffled by the situation. Scuba gear? Even if he could get some gear, would he be allowed to swim or dive in the area near the *Mayflower II*? How else could he see what was beneath the water? He was completely perplexed.

He was also extremely warm. It was a hot, summer day. He decided to head back to the campground and hit the pool for a while. It would refresh him, and then he would try to come at this problem from another angle.

The swim invigorated him. After changing back into his clothes, he decided to research some more information about the bay itself. He had been correct in assuming that the bay had undergone change since the arrival of the Pilgrims. Various sites mentioned dredging of the harbor area. This was not news that Harley had hoped to find.

If heavy machinery had been used, then it would be logical to assume that at some point the dredging had moved or removed the boulder that Hopkins had mentioned. It was highly likely that the clue Harley needed was no longer even in the bay. Not a comforting thought.

Harley decided to check on the latest volcanic activity from across the ocean. There were updates every couple of minutes and from the looks of it, the volcano seemed primed to erupt at any moment. There was even a live feed, much like the one used for the Old Faithful geyser at Yellowstone National Park.

Harley bookmarked that particular page, wanting the activity to be at his fingertips if necessary. Then he decided to make dinner over the fire. He wasn't in the mood for anything special, so he just grabbed a couple of hot dogs out of his cooler, along with some chips, fruit, and raw veggies. Once the fire was burning, it was only a few moments before the wieners began to sizzle on the pointed stick that Harley had fashioned.

Once the hot dogs were finished, Harley settled into his chair, enjoying the food and the quiet of the campground. While there were others throughout the campground, Harley's site was situated in such a manner that very few others were nearby. It made for a cozy setting, although a part of him wished he could share the experience. That got him thinking about Abby.

Over the past year he had not spoken to her, despite her repeated attempts to speak to him. Grandma had texted and spoken with Abby on various occasions. Grandma had told him that Abby had attended Chris's funeral, which Harley could not find within himself to attend. Meghan had been there, and the last thing Harley needed was another confrontation.

According to Grandma, who had spoken to Grandma Larson as well, Chris had been posthumously awarded a medal for his courageous act. The medal had been given to Chris's parents. Meghan was still devastated over the loss of Chris, especially since it had appeared that they might be able to start a life together.

Grandma Schultz related that Meghan had seen Abby, along with Grandma Larson, at the funeral. Meghan had not spoken to either of them, and had actually gone out of her way to avoid them. She was still filled with resentment. Being cheated out of a chance at happiness, even bliss, only to have it torn away at the last second, tends to infuriate even the nicest people. Harley shuddered, wondering if a year had been enough time for Meghan to heal. He doubted it, especially after Harley's episode with Abby's parents.

Revenge, misdirected or not, was always a possibility in Harley's mind, and while he didn't actually fear for his life, he would just as well like to avoid any unnecessary incidents. Harley was actually hopeful that at some point he would return to Virginia and visit Chris's grave. He was unsure if he could ever face Chris's family. He had sent condolences and flowers from Wisconsin, with help from Grandma, but he had never received any confirmation or thanks for them. Just as well, he wouldn't even know where to begin with any explanation that would make sense. Better to just leave well enough alone.

Harley shook his head and decided he should focus on the present situation, and the problem that presented itself. He had to figure out a way to find that elusive boulder that may hold the third amulet, and the key to solving the mystery, or even possibly the location, of Atlantis.

Realizing that his time might be limited, what with the possibility of a tsunami heading his way, he decided to research a little more about the destructive waves. Harley spent the next hour reading about their formation, earthquakes, landslides, crests, troughs, drawbacks, damage, speed, and anything else that might be useful.

Then, he decided he wanted to create a diagram of the first two amulets combined as one, so he hiked up to the lodge and asked if he could make a couple of copies on their machine. The desk worker allowed him some privacy, and he pulled out the copies of the two letters and the two amulets, and quickly ran them through the copier.

Once he grabbed the originals and the copies, he headed back to his site. He reached into the trailer and rummaged around until he found a pair of scissors. He carefully cut out the two shapes with the Greek letters, set them together, and placed a couple of pieces of scotch tape over them. Then he flipped over the taped pieces and examined the copies of the backsides. He had to match up the copies of the backsides to fit the front, and once he had that much done, he taped those in place as well.

Staring at the partially assembled puzzle, he began to consider what the pieces were trying to tell him. Something about the matching Greek letters on the front side bothered him. Abby had mentioned something about it previously, and he wondered what she may have been considering.

Harley punched *Greek alphabet* into his phone, and a website appeared with the now familiar shapes, along with their letters names and corresponding numbers.

"Alpha, 1," Harley started, "beta is 2, gamma is 3, delta is 4, epsilon is 5, digamma is 6, zeta is 7, eta is 8, and theta is 9. Hmmm."

Harley looked at the accompanying information, and he noted that the next nine letters corresponded with the multiples of 10 through 90. The last nine letters corresponded with the multiples of 100 through 900. He also noted that since the Greek alphabet had only 24 letters in Classic Greek, three additional characters were needed to complete the numbering system. Digamma, which was 6, koppa, which was 90, and sampi, which was 900, all came from archaic letters.

While he found this information interesting, as well as noting that many of the letters were used in fraternities and sororities, no help was forthcoming regarding the Atlantis mystery. There was, however, a cool application where he could insert names, and the site would tell the corresponding number.

Harley started with Atlantis, and the number was 892. He then tried his own name, and it came out as 144. Having found it intriguing, he began punching in name after name. Schultz equaled 1537, David, his dad, was 519, and Jennifer, his mom, was 730. Harley paused, and then he punched in Abby's name. He was surprised to see the number. 13. Unlucky 13? Could Abby be the key to all of this after all? Could all the filth he had spewed at her actually be dead on?

Emboldened, he Googled 13, and although he did not believe in numerology, he found that the number meant upheaval, so that new ground could be broken. He sat back on his haunches. Upheaval. Broken ground. Volcano equaled upheaval. Landslide equaled broken ground. This was becoming more alarming every moment.

He decided to look into his number, 144. He found that it was mentioned in the Bible in the book of Revelation. It was a measurement of part of celestial Jerusalem...heaven. He also found that Plato had mentioned the number 144. It meant that there would be great changes in cities every 144 years. 144 was also the square of 12, and Harley found it doubly interesting that the number 12 fell directly next to Abby's 13.

All of this was becoming too much for Harley to ingest. He finally turned off his phone, stood up, and headed to the restroom. He needed to relieve himself, and he needed to clear his head. The cool night air helped. He breathed deeply as he returned to his site. It was getting late, and deep down he knew that the morning was going to bring him just that much closer to the answers he sought, if not directly to the threshold. Harley crawled into the trailer, lay his head on his pillow, and in a matter of moments he was asleep.

The next morning Harley awoke to birds chirping and a soft breeze drifting through the trailer. Had he not been so committed to pursuing Atlantis, Harley probably would have pulled his sleeping bag back over him, rolled over, and gone back to sleep. It was one of those absolutely perfect summer mornings. No humidity, no dew wetting everything down, no irritating mosquitoes, just a beautiful morning that lent itself to happiness and harmony, not evil and destruction.

Harley clambered out of the trailer, grabbed his toiletry bag, and headed for the showers. He spent a few extra minutes letting the hot water stream over him, loosening up some tight muscles, then toweled off, dressed, and walked back to the trailer. He reached into his cooler, pulled out an apple, a granola bar, and a bottle of water. That would suffice until later. For now he wanted to head back down to Plymouth and survey the harbor again. He needed to come up with a plan.

Straddling his Road Glide, he fired the engine, released the clutch, and as quietly as the bike would allow, rumbled out of the campground and headed for town. Away from the campers, he squeezed the throttle, and the familiar growl of the V-twin roared to life. Harley settled back into the seat with a grin. "God, I love this," he said aloud. Freedom, fresh air, the open road, everything he desired was right here. Well, almost everything.

It was only a couple of minutes before he arrived down by Plymouth Rock and the park. He pulled into a parking area, shut down the motorcycle, and dismounted. Removing his helmet, he placed it on the passenger seat, in between his backrest and the touring pack.

Checking his phone, he found no messages, so he checked in on the volcanic activity across the ocean. Much to his surprise, there was a breaking story. In the past five hours, the volcano had begun to erupt, with more and more pressure being released from the vent. A dust and ash cloud was already miles into the air. Scientists were studying the seismographic information, as well as watching live feed cameras from both earth and space, searching for any movement that might suggest a part of the island was breaking apart, a precursor to a massive landslide.

Harley decided to wander around through the park, still searching for an idea that would solve his dilemma with the hidden boulder. He stared at the beach, noting the level of the water. It was easily a couple feet lower than he recalled the previous time he had been there. Much more of the beach was exposed, many small rocks were evident. This got Harley thinking, and slowly, almost imperceptibly, a plan was evolving. It was a risky plan, a plan involving exquisite timing, a plan that could result in Harley's own destruction, but a plan nevertheless.

He again checked his phone, noting when high tide and low tide took place in Plymouth harbor. He noted that it was low tide right now, almost the lowest it would be all month. Then he switched over to the volcano watch. From the most recent update and images, it would only be a matter of time until the volcano really blew its top. Then it was just a matter of a piece of the island either sliding into the Atlantic, or absolutely nothing occurring, other than the eruption itself.

Harley decided to check out other tourist attractions, since it seemed he was now in wait mode. He chose the Jenney Grist Mill, in part because he had wanted to visit it the previous year with Abby and Chris, and in part because it was just down the road, and Harley wanted to stay downtown for most of the day, just in case he had to put his plan into motion.

The Jenney Grist Mill was actually a very enjoyable tour. The workers showed him, and others who had taken the tour, how the entire process worked, including the stopping and starting of the water flow, which was the power source. From there, the workers explained the process of lining up the grinding stones, and then they ran some grain through, with the end result being flour that could be used for any number of baking needs.

Harley once again found himself marveling at the workers' knowledge and humorous anecdotes as they continued the process. Every time Harley visited a re-enactment site-Roanoke, Jamestown, Williamsburg, and now Plymouth-he came away with a much deeper respect for what early Americans had to do to survive, as well as the ingenious inventions from those days. With no electricity, water power was one of very few options, along with windmills, to provide a source of energy to do work.

After touring the mill, Harley decided to grab a bite to eat at one of the local cafes. When he finished, he decided to take a different perspective, and get out on the water. There was a whale watching tour just down the street from the *Mayflower II*, so he walked down there, purchased a ticket, and then waited a short while until the crew was ready for the passengers to board.

The weather was almost perfect as they pulled away from the dock, headed out along the break wall, passing by the *Mayflower II* and the Plymouth Rock Memorial. It was quite a view from the boat, and Harley took some time to snap few photos along the way.

As they headed out into open water, the shoreline began to recede into the distance. Harley continued to note landmarks in the town, as well as photograph them in case he needed some markers in the future.

Before long they were well away from shore, and Harley turned away from land and began to search the area for whales. He did not have long to wait. The captain and crew announced that they were in the midst of an excellent whale watching season, and almost on cue, a whale breached just off the side of the boat, landing with a glorious splash that had the tourists, Harley included, cheering and pointing.

Moments later another whale spouted, and again there was an excited frenzy of voices on the boat as the passengers scrambled to get a good view and snap as many photos as they could. This continued for quite a while, and Harley found himself somewhat exhausted by the time they headed back into port.

After an eventful morning and afternoon, Harley was feeling hungry. As he disembarked from the boat, he decided to head straight back to camp for the night and prepare some dinner. He had some burgers sitting in the cooler, and once he had the campfire burning, he could quickly grill a couple of them. Grabbing a few odds and ends to devour along with them, he could then relax for the evening. Even though he was playing a waiting game, he wasn't about to sit around and do nothing. The pool and hot tub beckoned.

After he finished his meal, he banked the fire, changed into his swim trunks, and strolled over to the pool. There was an air of excitement as the people that were sunbathing all seemed to be discussing the volcano that was now making national news. Harley heard one couple say that they were heading out in the morning, leaving nothing to chance should the worst scenario occur. Others were taking a wait and see approach. After all, 8 hours was plenty of time to get a few miles inland, which would be what was necessary to avoid being caught up in the disaster.

Not wanting to dwell on the negative, yet at the same time knowing the eruption was integral to his plan, Harley began swimming laps in the pool, avoiding the smaller children as he cruised along. The more he swam, the more energy he seemed to have, so he just kept going, losing count of how many laps he made. Finally, he stopped to catch his breath. As he pulled himself from the pool, he knew he would sleep well that night. Open ocean whale watching for hours, plus a long swim, had finally drained him.

He returned to his fire, which had dwindled down to just a few embers. He was able to procure some tinder, relight the fire, and then toss a couple larger pieces of wood onto the blaze. Then he changed out of his wet trunks, threw on a pair of shorts and a T shirt, and settled down in his bag-in-a-chair. Reaching for his phone, he continued to monitor the goings on across the ocean.

The volcanic activity was growing stronger every hour, the reports said, and scientists were predicting a large explosion in the next 24-48 hours. Harley nodded his head at the news, and then decided he should probably let his grandma know what was going on.

He texted a message to Grandma Schultz, telling her that he was in Plymouth, and yes, he was watching the news. Then he filled her in on the events of the day, hoping she would see his visit to the mill and the whale watching as a sign that he was doing more touring than investigating. He knew she would still be worried, so Harley did his best to keep a light tone to his message, at least what was possible in a text. He even placed a smiley face at the end of the message, hoping it would placate her.

Grandma returned the text almost immediately. Harley grinned, believing that she had probably been staring at her phone, willing it to ring or buzz. She needed to know that her prodigal grandson was still alive and well. Her message was cryptic. "Please leave the area in the morning. It's too dangerous." Then on a lighter note, "Glad you had fun whale watching." It was followed by an emoticon winking at him. You had to love Grandma Schultz. Even in a serious situation, she tried to remain light-hearted.

Harley texted again. He told her that he would check in with her in the morning, and that he was about to jump in the trailer and go to sleep. She messaged him a good night, and then Harley placed the phone in the trailer, sat down by the fire, and just stared at it as the flames dwindled. His thoughts turned to his mom and dad.

He missed them terribly. He wished there was a way he could be together again with them. Thinking of the upcoming possibilities, he sighed. It was very possible that by this time tomorrow, or maybe the next day, he could very well be reunited with them. Of course, he believed they were in heaven, as they had been God-fearing people who had extremely strong faiths. Considering what words he had uttered in the past year, of the blasphemies he had screamed at God, he was for the moment uncertain about a reunion. He might be heading in the other direction. He shuddered at that thought.

Still, he thought, was God deliberately testing him, or was this some evil force that was attempting to crush his spirit? It was easy to blame God, but considering all the secrets he had kept, it was quite possible that his own pride had gotten in the way. *Pride goeth before the fall.* That proverb from the Bible continued to peck away at his inner being.

Another sigh. Well, he had promised his mother that he would see this through, even though she in no way had ever requested that he do so. Despite that, he would continue his search, regardless of the outcome.

As he stared at the fire, he began to nod off. He roused himself enough to spread out the ashes, fold up the chair, and crawl inside the trailer. He was out almost as soon as his head hit the pillow. For the first time in a long time, he slept soundly, never once waking until morning.

Meanwhile, across the ocean, just before dawn on the East Coast, La Palma finally erupted with a roar. Minutes later, a huge chunk on the western side of the island, facing directly at America, slid into the ocean. The tsunami was on its way.

⸺»《◍》«⸺

Harley awoke to the sounds of excited voices and campers being readied for departure. As he poked his head out of the trailer, he was shocked to see the mad scramble of campers as they frantically gathered their belongings, tore down temporary shelters, and hollered at one another to hurry. All this commotion could mean only one thing.

Harley clicked on his phone and immediately searched for information on the volcano. It had indeed erupted, and much to his amazement, and horror, a huge sheet of the island had slid into the sea. The report indicated that this had occurred about an hour earlier.

Harley did some quick calculating. The distance was a little over 3000 miles from La Palma to Plymouth. If the tsunami was traveling at about 500 miles per hour, then it would arrive in about six hours. He had slept through the first hour, and seeing that the time on his phone said 7:00 a.m., he realized that the first wave should hit around 12 noon.

Harley knew it was now or never. He had to set his plan in motion. He quickly closed up the trailer, placing all of his belongings either in the trailer or in the motorcycle. Hooking the trailer to the bike, he was ready for departure in less than 15 minutes.

Harley stopped at the office long enough to let them know he was leaving. He wished the owners well, and they in turn told him to be careful. People would be in a hurry, and a motorcycle was certainly at a higher risk today above all days.

Harley took this all in stride. Traffic was heading away from Plymouth and the shoreline. He decided to pick up I-495 and head up toward Middleborough Center. It was there he would drop off the trailer at a hotel parking lot and then return to Plymouth.

After he unhooked the trailer, Harley headed up to Highway 44 and backtracked to Plymouth. There was almost no one on his side of the road as he approached the town. Realizing that the police and National Guard could very well be directing traffic away from town, he decided to follow some of the back streets through the town, and park near Burial Hill. He wanted a view of the harbor, as well as having his motorcycle pointed in the right direction if he needed a quick getaway, which he was sure would be a necessity.

Timing was going to be everything. It was only a couple of blocks down the hill to the water's edge. He could sprint there in less than a minute, which was about all the time he would be able to spare. Then the real challenge would begin. Find the amulet and escape before the enormous waves closed in over him.

Harley parked the bike on the corner of Leyden Street and Main Street. It seemed appropriate he was right next to the location of Stephen Hopkins' home. If all went as planned, he would make it to his bike, make a quick left on Market Street, merge onto Summer Street, and then pray his V-Twin could get him to Pilgrims Highway, a little over half a mile away. If he could reach that spot, he might be safe from the wall of water. He didn't plan on stopping there, but that was his goal.

Harley dismounted, pulling off his helmet and storing it under his bungee web that held down his sleeping bag. Running with a helmet on would only slow him down, and he would need every inch if he was going to pull this off. For now, he hiked up to Burial Hill, looked down on the bay, and chose to take a seat next to William Bradford's stone monument. It had been set back in place since the last time Harley had been here. Thinking about what was to occur, he shook his head at the waste.

"Might as well have left them all laying on their sides," he said aloud. "In a few hours, they will all be gone anyway."

Harley found an area in the graveyard where he could remain somewhat hidden from the police or anyone else still left in the town, and yet he was still able to see the bay clearly. He was also looking straight down Leyden Street, and he could see his motorcycle parked in the distance. With all the commotion that was going on, Harley was somewhat concerned that looters would be about, and they might possibly damage the bike.

Fortunately, there were quite few police vehicles patrolling the streets, so he felt relatively secure in the knowledge that his bike would make it through unscathed, at least until the wave showed up. Then all bets were off.

Harley had grabbed a bottle of water, an energy bar, and an apple before trekking up to the cemetery. After sitting a while, he checked the time. It was about 10:00. He decided to break into his little stash and eat something. He was getting warm as the sun rose higher in the sky, so the water was a welcome treat. There was no sense in starving himself or suffering dehydration. He would need every ounce of strength and speed to pull this off, if it was even possible at all.

He continued to observe the action in town from his perch in the cemetery. Occasionally he would see people running down the street. The police and National Guard were ever vigilant, and Harley was proud and despondent simultaneously. Those men and women were placing their lives in jeopardy to save lives and property. Yet, once the waves came, all the property would be destroyed. At least no one would profit from the misfortune of others.

Seeing all the law enforcement on the streets concerned Harley. What would happen once he made a dash for the beach? He hoped that all of the people left in town would have cleared out by the time he needed to make his dash for the beach. After all, they were not going to stay if the town had been evacuated. That would be suicide. As the morning wore on, it appeared to Harley as if less and less people were on the streets.

By 11:00 it was nearly deserted. An occasional vehicle, lights flashing, would drive down Main Street. Harley noted that no one had gone near his motorcycle, and he was grateful for that. One police car had stopped by it earlier, given it the once over, and continued on. Other vehicles had been left behind on the streets as well, as tourists and townspeople alike headed for safety. Possessions could be replaced. Lives could not.

It was about 11:30. Harley stood up and stretched, still keeping himself as hidden as he could. He began to limber up as if preparing for a sporting event. The last thing he needed was a cramp or a hamstring pull on his sprint down and back up the hill. He continued to stretch over and over, legs then arms, twisting his torso, shrugging the tightness out of his shoulders. He was glad at this moment that he had been an athlete throughout high school. He was in excellent shape, and if this plan of his was going to have any success, athletic agility and stamina would be a must.

Finally, the time on his phone read 12:00. It was time to put his plan into action. He glanced at the bay. The water was still, with no change from the last hour. The tide was slowly beginning to go out, but the lower tide appeared minimal. Harley did not want to be caught out in the open, fearing that the police would haul him away for his own good. Still, with so little movement on the streets, he decided that to head down now would allow him a little extra time once he reached the beach.

Harley began his sprint down Leyden Street, passing by his beloved motorcycle with nary a glance. He sprinted right across Water Street and alongside where Town Brook emptied into the bay. The marina was just to the right of Harley as he pulled up alongside the break wall that ran along Pilgrim Memorial State Park. He climbed over the rocks stealthily, and in a few moments stood along the deserted shoreline.

The *Mayflower II* was nowhere in sight. Harley knew from reading up on tsunamis that if a boat was just a few miles away from shore, the waves would only be gentle swells passing under it. It was when the bottom of the sea became shallow that the waves slowed down, piled up, and then came crashing onto the shore. He guessed the replica ship was now far out at sea.

Harley stood there waiting, hoping against hope that he was right, and the opportunity he had envisioned would materialize. It was deathly quiet. No waves even washed up on the beach. That was why he was so startled when heard a voice behind him whisper softly, "Do you really think the drawback is going to allow you enough time to find what you're looking for?"

———————◦((◦))◦———————

If Harley Schultz had heard it once from his parents, he had heard it a thousand times. *The best laid plans often go awry.* "Why today, God? Why today?"

Harley turned around slowly, and there she was. Long, silky hair, tied in a ponytail, unbelievably smooth, tanned skin, white halter top, blue jeans, and running shoes. "Thank God, she isn't wearing sandals," Harley thought.

The most beautiful eyes Harley had ever seen in his life, along with the smile that would forever hold him captive, peered up at him.

Abby.

"What are you doing here?" Harley gasped. "Do you want to get yourself killed?"

"I was going to ask you the same thing," Abby replied quietly, never once taking her eyes from his. "But you still didn't answer my question. Do you think the drawback will be long enough for you to find what you're looking for?"

"What do you know about drawback?" Harley asked, stunned by both Abby's presence, and the fact that she seemed to know his exact plan.

"I know that when there is a tsunami, often there will be a drawback of water into the ocean. It's the trough before the first crest of the tsunami, or any wave for that matter, but in a tsunami the water can drawback hundreds of yards into the ocean, and remains that way for many minutes. My guess is you suspect something is out in the bay, and you're waiting for the water to drawback so you can go search. How am I doing so far?" Abby asked, a bit petulantly.

"Where did you come from?" Harley asked, now even more amazed by Abby's unexpected appearance and analysis of the whole situation.

Abby shook her head. "Nuh-uh, you first. Tell me what's going on. I deserve an explanation. I haven't seen you in a year, quite possibly the worst year of my life, thank you very little. You owe me." She stood defiantly, hands on hips, eyes never wavering from her continued gaze into Harley's eyes, his soul.

If the situation had not been so dangerous, and the last year not been so devastating, Harley would have laughed at Abby's posturing. As it was, he had no choice but to start at the beginning and explain what had occurred the previous year.

"Okay, you're right. I am hoping for the drawback of the ocean. I'm hoping to find a boulder that holds the third and final amulet. It will probably give me, us, the location of Atlantis."

Despite her wariness and determination, a hint of a smile appeared on Abby's beautiful face. "Us," she whispered. "You do care about me. I knew it!" However, just as quickly she appeared businesslike and resolute. "What boulder are you talking about? You're talking in riddles."

For an answer, Harley pulled out the Stephen Hopkins' letter and handed it wordlessly to Abby. She scanned it quickly, looked back into Harley's eyes, and asked, "Where did you get this?"

Harley took a deep breath and sat down on a large rock. "The day I took off from the police station, something, some force, I don't even know how to explain it, led me back to Burial Hill. There were all kinds of damage from the flash flood and storm. Grave markers were tipped over…and graves were disturbed. I mean, really disturbed."

"You found this by a grave?" asked Abby incredulously.

Harley nodded. "Not just any grave, but I believe it was Stephen Hopkins' unmarked grave. How else would I have found a letter written in his own hand?"

Abby turned her attention back to the letter. As she stared at it, her eyes widened. "The shape! It sort of looks like a wave!"

"Then you see it too," Harley commented wryly. "At least I'm not completely crazy."

Abby returned her gaze to Harley's face, "Yes, you are. You left me without any explanation. You found another clue to Atlantis and told no one. Now you are standing next to a shoreline that will soon be inundated by a tsunami, hoping that you will have enough time to find a boulder that may or may not be here, all in the off chance of finding a long lost continent just so you can keep a promise you made to your mother, who wasn't even alive when you made it! I would say that makes you completely crazy!"

Harley was having difficulty determining if the tone of her voice was serious, mocking, or joking. She sounded angry, with good reason, no doubt, but still Harley could sense a small amount of tongue-in cheek mischief in her demeanor. However, the fact that a tsunami was heading directly toward them at the speed of a jet airliner kept Harley focused on the danger. The gravity of the situation allowed no time for humor.

"Okay," Harley conceded, "I was way off base, and I'm sorry, Abby. I truly am, but we are in an extremely dangerous predicament, one that I tried my best to keep you from, and yet you are still here. Now, quickly, how did you get here, and more importantly, why are you here?"

Realization poured over Abby's face. "You broke up with me because you didn't want anything to happen to me? That's what this is all about? How could you do that, after all we've been through. Just like you, I have the right to make my own decisions. Now I'm really mad!"

"Yes, yes, you have every right to be mad, Abby. Just not now! Do you understand the danger we are in? Now tell me how and why you are here, and if anyone else we care about is here or knows what either of us is up to."

Abby was actually taken aback for a moment by Harley's forcefulness. She stammered, "Grandma Schultz told me you were heading here. I've been in touch with her ever since you went to Wisconsin. When you left Bennington, I decided to come here on my own. I got in yesterday."

"And you just so happened to show up here, at this spot, right now?"

Abby blushed. "Well, no, not exactly. I sort of have been following you for the past day or so. I was a Marine kid, remember. I followed you to the Triple C, was able to find a site on the other side of the campground, and kept an eye on you until you went to bed. Then I tailed you into town, and parked up by the other cemeteries, and spied on you up at Burial Hill. Once you took off down the hill, I just followed you as quickly as I could."

Abby was nearly beet red after admitting she had been spying on him for the past 12-24 hours. Harley, on the other hand, couldn't decide if he was more angry or amazed at this particular revelation. Here he thought he had been so clever, and Abby had outfoxed him at every turn.

"All right," Harley took a deep breath, "so here we both are. Let's plan this out as best we can. I'm praying that the drawback occurs, and it will allow us time to find the boulder and the amulet. I think the third amulet will fit together with the other two and make a map of some sort. Here, let me show you what I made last night, unless of course you already know."

Abby blushed again. "No, I didn't see everything you did. Show me."

Harley pulled out the taped amulet pieces and allowed Abby to examine them. She flipped them over and over again. "They sure do seem to fit together. If we find the third one, it should clear up an awful lot, don't you think?"

"Hopefully everything," Harley agreed, "I would really like for this to be over, one way or another."

Abby didn't particularly like that notion, but rather than start any kind of argument, she decided it was prudent to remain focused on the search for the final amulet. "So what is your plan, exactly?"

Harley explained, "If the drawback occurs, we head out into the bay, see if we can find the boulder, grab the amulet, and run like heck. I've got the motorcycle pointed in the right direction, and I'm just hoping to make it back up the hill before the waves reach here."

"How long do drawbacks last?" Abby asked.

"It depends, anywhere from a few seconds to five or six minutes. The bigger the wave, the longer the trough and crest. If this is a mega-tsunami, I'm guessing between five and ten minutes. Not a whole lot of time."

Abby stared out over the bay. The water had yet to recede, so she decided that since she had a few moments, she would like some clarification on a few things.

"So, you're bound and determined to see this through, no matter what the outcome?"

Harley nodded, "Yes," he said quietly.

"Even if I could die in all of this?"

"You weren't supposed to be here!" Harley began to protest.

Abby held up her hands as if in self-defense. "I know, I know. That was unfair to say. I'm sorry." She took a deep breath. "I am here now, and I plan on seeing this through also, come hell or high water."

"My thoughts exactly," Harley responded, amazed that she had echoed his own words.

"So where do you think we should look? It's a big bay, so a boulder, if it's still here, could be difficult to find."

"The bay has been dredged before, so it is possible that the boulder is gone. You're right about that, but I'm guessing that most of the dredging was done over by the *Mayflower II*, and along the beach by Plymouth Rock. Something tells me that since Hopkins lived on Leyden Street, and he could look out over the bay from there, maybe the boulder is somewhere over here by the marina. It's just a guess, but we may as well start here as anywhere."

Abby smiled again at the word *we*, but did not comment on it. She did agree with Harley's reasoning though. "Plymouth wasn't all that big when he was alive, so why wouldn't he have noticed the boulder straight off the shore. Still, how was he able to see it? Wouldn't the sea level have been more or less the same as now? What would have made the boulder suddenly appear?"

Harley considered that question for a moment. Then he replied, "When the Pilgrims arrived here, it was during a mini ice age. That would mean more water would be locked up in the polar regions as ice, which could lower the sea level significantly."

"That makes sense," Abby agreed. "It would give Hopkins access to more of the bay, so hopefully the boulder has been left undisturbed since then." Another thought occurred to her. "If there's one boulder, doesn't that mean there could be more, maybe many more?"

Harley nodded. He had thought the same thing.

"So how do we know what we're looking for?" Abby asked.

Harley shrugged.

"Oh, you're a big help," Abby said mockingly. "Great, so we're going to wander around the bay, looking for a boulder that could be anywhere, shaped like anything, and we have a tsunami coming. Maybe I'm the crazy one!"

Harley finally smiled at her. He couldn't control it, or what he said next, "Well, you're certainly not the sharpest tool in the shed."

"*What?*"

Harley grinned at her. "I'm obviously more intelligent than you. After all, you chose me, which probably wasn't the smartest move in history, and I chose you, which makes me look like a genius."

It took Abby a moment to realize he was messing with her, and once she regained her composure, she just shook her head and retorted, "You didn't choose me. I just let you hang out with me. Kind of like I was taking in a stray puppy that had lost its way." She grinned that mischievous smile that Harley adored.

Harley returned Abby's barb with a whimpering, puppy-like sound. "Please, Miss Abby, take me home with you," he needled.

"More like take you to the pound, since I haven't been able to train you properly. I thought I had complete control over you. I must be slipping in my old age."

Harley laughed, "You still do pretty well...for an old lady."

Abby was about to come back with another witty retort when she stopped short. The look on her face had changed from frolic to frown. Harley instantly noticed the difference, and his demeanor changed just as rapidly. "What's wrong, Abby?"

Abby simply pointed to the water. "It's starting," she stated, her voice that had a moment before been so upbeat, was now strained with fear.

Harley reached over and took her hand in his. "Whatever happens, I want you to know that I love you, Abby. I've never said it, but it's true. So much so that I could not bear the thought of losing you to this...curse, or whatever it is."

Abby's eyes began watering immediately. "I love you, too, Harley." She threw herself into his arms, and in a moment when all the world could come crashing down on top of them, their lips met with a passion neither had felt before.

Common sense overcame desire, however, and Harley gently pulled away just long enough to whisper, "Just remember I said it first."

Abby groaned aloud, "I'll never live that down, if I live at all," she finished wryly. She pulled away from Harley and stepped toward the sea.

"Right," Harley agreed, "let's get to work. We don't have much time."

Whatever Atlantis had in store for them, it would be over in the next 15 minutes.

———◦《◦》◦———

The sea began to recede from the shoreline, and Harley and Abby immediately began to follow the waterline just as quickly as they could, all the while scanning back and forth for any sign of a boulder that might suddenly materialize and beckon them.

They were well beyond the marina when a number of boulders began to appear. Harley glanced back at the shore to find his bearings. He was using Leyden Street as his guide, believing that Hopkins had indeed seen something in the bay from his own doorway.

He noticed that he had veered a little to his left, so he retraced his steps and began scrutinizing boulders that fell along that track. Abby was sprinting back and forth, stopping at as many boulders as she could reach, searching in vain for any sign that they were on the right path.

Harley called out, "Three minutes," as he glanced at his phone and noted the time. Abby stopped long enough to meet his eyes and nod. Harley saw the growing terror and helplessness, and he couldn't help himself. "Abby, please get out of here. There's no need for you to do this."

"Shut up and keep looking!"

"You're still beautiful," Harley called to her again.

"And you're still cute. Keep searching!" she ordered.

Harley grinned despite the peril. It was then he looked down at a very large boulder which he needed to circumvent because of its size. As he reached the far side of the huge rock, he came face to face with the clue he sought.

There, hammered into the rock, were the same nine Greek letters that appeared on the two amulets. "Abby! Come here! I found it!" he cried triumphantly.

Abby sprinted there in a matter of moments, staring in awe at the symbols that they had so often observed. The letters formed a circle around a small opening in the rock, just large enough to place one's hand. Harley began to reach for the opening when Abby grabbed his arm. "Harley, what if there's something dangerous in there?"

He grinned and said, "A tsunami is bearing down on us, and you are worried that some little crab or crayfish might grab my finger? I'll take my chances."

As he reached again for the opening, Abby mumbled, "Sure, say 'I love you' one time, and you become Mr. Cocky."

It was not a straight opening, but rather one that required Harley to snake his hand upward and then slightly to the right. As he scraped his knuckles on the stone, he felt something move freely inside the crevice. He fingered the object, pulling it toward him gingerly. As he retracted his arm and finally his hand, he was able to finally pull the object out into the sunlight.

They gasped at what they beheld. It was another golden amulet, and it was shaped exactly like a wave, just as Harley had predicted.

"Look at the letters!" he gasped. "Just like the other two, see? Alpha beta, gamma, delta, epsilon, digamma, zeta, eta, theta." Harley caressed each symbol as he spoke them.

Harley glanced at Abby as he finished, and instead of seeing an expression of happiness and excitement, there was only alarm.

"Oh, my God!" Abby cried out. "Oh, my God! Oh, my God! Oh my God!" Abby's voice level had reached almost a shriek.

"Abby, what's wrong?" Harley was aghast at her reaction.

She grabbed his arm. "Harley, tell me exactly what your dad said before he died. Please!"

"What?" Harley could not understand how Abby had gone off

on such a tangent.

"Hurry, what did he say?"

Harley was not about to argue, so he simply stated, "He said, 'Harley, they', and then he said, 'Harley, they da.' Those were his last words. What does that have to do with anything?"

Abby had turned white with fear. She appeared as if she would burst out crying. She kept her composure, albeit with great difficulty, and explained through gasps, "Harley, he wasn't saying they da, he was trying to say *theta!*"

"Why would he say that?"

"Harley, do you remember when I told you that something about the letters and their arrangement was bothering me?"

Harley nodded quickly, and Abby continued with another odd request, "Let me see those two pieces that you taped together." Harley yanked them out of his pocket, laid them on the rock, and placed the newest amulet next to them. It was a perfect fit! The three were supposed to be together.

Harley quickly flipped them over, and as he placed the amulet next to the paper versions of the others, his eyes widened in disbelief. "Oh, my God, Abby! We found it! We found Atlantis! It's right there, plain as day! My mom was right!" He looked up at the heavens and shouted, "You were right, Mom! You were right! It does exist! Atlantis is for real, and now we can prove it!"

He was so excited that he even started to do a little jig, but as he spun around he caught sight of Abby, and her troubled, daresay frantic, appearance halted Harley mid-step.

"Harley, we have to go now! And we need to leave the amulet behind. The papers and letters too. All of it!"

"*What? Are you nuts?*"

"Harley, please listen. Don't interrupt. Just listen, please!"

Abby's hysteria caused him to freeze just as he was about to start an argument. Harley could do nothing but nod and murmur, "Go ahead. Talk."

Abby was nearly hyperventilating. "Harley, your dad wrote in his notes about Plato, number/letter relationship, and symbolism."

She paused to take a breath and continued, "The Greeks didn't have the number system we do. They only used nine numbers, and symbolically they mean completeness."

She gasped for another breath of air. "Alpha also means beginning, like in the Bible where it says God is the Alpha and the Omega, but your dad said theta, and theta means death, Harley. If you put all of these things together, with Alpha starting at the beginning of each amulet, and theta at the end, or the core of each, then from alpha to theta translates into the beginning of complete and utter death and destruction. Bringing the three together, even with two of them being paper, fulfills the curse."

Abby had to stop. Her breathing was becoming erratic, Harley was alarmed at the possibility that she might pass out, and he knew he would never make it to safety if he had to carry her.

Meanwhile, his mind was spinning, attempting to decipher all that Abby had so quickly thrown at him. While it all made sense, especially with all the death and destruction that had occurred thus far, Harley was hesitant to just drop everything and leave. He had spent too much time, and had lost far too much, to just let it go.

"Abby, we know where Atlantis is. How can I break my promise to my mom when I finally have all the answers?"

"You already fulfilled your promise, Harley. You proved that Atlantis is real, but if we continue, then the curse will be fulfilled as well…and we will die. We may, anyway, if we don't leave now. It's been ten minutes. The tsunami is coming. If we don't leave now, we will die. Harley, I don't want to die! I want to live! I want to live with you! I love you! Please believe me! I know I'm right, and I know your dad was trying to warn you to stop. Please, let it go!"

Harley paused for a moment. A piece of him wanted to lash out at her with some smart aleck comment, that he wasn't about to let it go. Thankfully, the stronger part of him, the part that his parents had instilled in him from the time he was a toddler, the part that truly believed that love beat hate, that good defeated evil, that God triumphed over Satan, ultimately rose to the surface.

"Okay, Abby. I believe you. I did fulfill my promise to my mom. We did discover the truth about Atlantis. My grandma was right. It's more important that I am happy and that I find fulfillment in my life, and not with this curse either."

He stared at the amulet again, as it lay there reunited with the pseudo amulets, when a sudden insight halted him. "They weren't trying to find Atlantis."

Abby stared at him in surprise. "What?"

"We were all wrong. Why would they split them up and hide them if the goal was to find Atlantis? Looking at them, they must have known where it was located."

"So why, then?"

"They knew it was cursed, and they didn't have the ability or resources to handle it. Still, they didn't want to just get rid of the amulets, in case future generations could figure it out, so they just split them up, and then left clues for others to find, in hope that one day Atlantis could be 'rediscovered' without any harm coming."

Abby was stunned at this development, but she also knew that time was of the essence, so she responded, "I think you're right, Harley, but we need to go. Now!"

Harley took one more longing gaze at the talisman and asked, "Do you want to take one last look at this? Only you and I will ever know the location of Atlantis." He held out the wave-shaped amulet and the taped shapes of the tornado and hurricane.

Abby stared at the map that the three combined pieces clearly revealed. She shook her head, "Who would have thought it was there? Sometimes the truth is staring you right in the face."

Harley gently pulled the amulet and papers from her hand, reached into his pocket and retrieved his other notes from the past investigations, folded the amulet into the center of all those pieces of paper, and slid them back into the crevice in the large boulder. Turning to Abby, he asked, "Are you okay, now?"

Abby had calmed down. "Yeah, I think so."

"Good, because we're not out of this yet. Run, Abby! Run!"

Abby and Harley sprinted out from behind the boulder and ran directly toward Leyden Street. The sea bottom was mucky, and it slowed their progress. As they reached the beach and scaled the break wall, a roar could be heard behind them. They never even paused to look, but continued their sprint up the incline that was Leyden Street, straining to reach Harley's motorcycle and praying that they would be able to outrun the monster wave that was bearing down on them.

Harley pulled ahead of Abby, reaching into his pocket for the key that he had used to lock the front end of his bike. He needed to reach the bike before her, unlock it, and have it fired and ready to tear away as soon as she scrambled onto the passenger seat. Taking a page out of his father's book, he had prepared for this event. Being proactive might very well save his life.

Harley dove onto his Road Glide, slammed the key in the lock, clicked the lock off and into the "on" position, yanked the clutch with his left hand, pushed the Start button with his right, and simultaneously kicked the side stand into the up position. The beast roared to life just as Abby grabbed his left shoulder and propelled her leg up and over the touring pack and landed smack dab in the middle of her seat.

Harley popped the clutch, gunned the throttle, and the front end jumped off the ground as the rear tire grabbed the pavement and shot them forward. Harley very nearly lost it, but he was able to maintain his balance, and as the front tire hit the pavement, he immediately leaned hard left and wheeled onto Market Street, just as he had planned. Knowing that there would be no traffic, and needing to move as swiftly as possible, he did not bother to stay in his own lane, rather he cut the corner much like a dirt track racer or a NASCAR driver would do.

The sharp lean to the left was followed immediately by another sharp lean and turn to the right as Harley powered his way up Summer Street. He slammed through the gears in moments, and was up to 100 miles per hour in a matter of just a few seconds. He glanced only once into the mirror, and what he saw behind him was beyond description. A wall of water had struck the shore, and in that one short glance, he saw buildings completely shattered, as if struck by an atomic bomb.

He did not peek again, but rather leaned down over his jet black, six-gallon gas tank, and willed his bike to go faster. "C'mon, baby, you can do it. Go! Go! Go!"

They flew under Pilgrim's Highway, but Harley still did not feel safe. He continued at breakneck speed for another minute, which in effect was over two miles. He only once glanced at his speedometer, and it was pegged at 120 miles per hour.

Finally, Harley allowed himself to sneak another peek in his mirror. He could not see the giant wave anymore, but he knew from his research that the water could continue well inland. He was not going to stop just yet. He did, however, release his death grip from the throttle and slowed the bike down to a mere 70 miles per hour, which was still well above the posted speed limit. Harley was more than willing to pay for a speeding ticket, should some insanely suicidal police officer pull him over.

Another mile passed, then another. Summer Street had actually changed names along the way. As he passed a cross street, Harley noted that it was now called Federal Furnace Road. He wound through the area, gradually bringing the Road Glide down to the posted speed limit signs, but he did not stop until he reached the I-495 exchange. Even then, he continually was glancing behind him, fearing that the wave could make it this far inland.

Harley pulled under the viaduct, pulled off to the side of the road, and came to a stop. He shut down the engine, and kicked the side stand down into position to hold up the heavy bike. It was only then he realized that Abby had a death grip around his waist. He gently caressed her arms, and pulled them apart, which allowed her to shakily dismount. He followed, just as erratically. They both collapsed on the incline of the underpass.

Adrenaline in one's body allows it to do superhuman feats, but once the action is over, the body nears complete exhaustion. Both of them had reached that point. They lay there next to each other, gasping and breathing heavily.

Finally, Abby was able to utter, "Well, that was fun."

Harley snorted. Abby giggled. Harley began laughing. Abby's giggles turned to guffaws, and soon neither of them could control their joy and relief. Every time they looked at each other, another burst of laughter echoed from under the highway. Tears streamed down their faces, and finally they were able to compose themselves.

"I've never been so scared in all my life," Abby finally managed. "My eyes were screwed shut the entire time you were driving until I felt you let off the throttle. I kept waiting for the water to catch us and pull us under."

Harley was spent. He laid there, eyes closed, listening to the sweet sounds of Abby's voice, and just smiled. "What are you grinning about?" Abby asked, pulling herself over to him and peering down.

"Just happy to be alive. Happy to be with you." He stopped for a moment, opened his eyes, and then propped himself up on his elbows. Abby noted a worried look on his face. "I am... with you, aren't I?" he asked, a bit apprehensively. After all he had put this beautiful, young woman through, she could easily tell him to take a hike.

Abby felt the balance of power shifting back in her favor, and she coyly smiled at him. "Oh, I suppose I'll keep you around for a while. I do love little lost puppies." With that little dig, she rolled onto him, forcing him back flat onto the ground. "After all, you did say you loved me."

"Guess I'll never live that down," Harley smiled at her. "Looks like I'll have to spend the rest of my life proving that I mean it."

"The rest of your life," Abby murmured. "I like the sound of that. You might as well get started right away then."

"Meaning?"

"Meaning, kiss me like you mean it. Now!"

"Yes, boss."

———— ❖ ————

"Reporting live from Boston, in an unprecedented event, Mother Nature has once again flexed her muscle, proving that mankind is no match for her. The tsunami, caused by the volcanic eruption in the Canary Islands and eventual landslide, arrived on our shores at about noon eastern time. Massive damage has been experienced up and down the eastern seaboard."

The announcer paused to catch his breath, while the cameraman revealed some of the damage in a sweeping view of the seashore.

The broadcast continued, "Reports from up and down the coast indicate that while damage was extensive, scientists were pleasantly surprised that it was not much worse. In a seemingly unexplained phenomenon, much of the energy from the wave dissipated just as it drew inland. Water levels were nowhere near as high as previously expected."

Another panoramic view by the cameraman made viewers gasp. Many places were leveled. If this wasn't as severe as expected, what would it have been like in a worst case scenario?

"The worst damage seems to have been isolated to three specific areas, the Outer Banks in North Carolina, the Historic Triangle near Jamestown, Virginia, and Plymouth Harbor, just outside of Boston. Coincidentally, the first two locations were also the settings of the two Atlantis discoveries that made national news over the past couple of years. Reporters in those two locations stated that the buildings that held the ancient relics were destroyed by monster waves, and all information regarding the lost civilization of Atlantis was lost to the sea. And now, in other news…"

Harley reached over and grabbed Abby's hand as they sat together in a booth at a café well inland from the inundated areas along the coast. "Are you okay?"

Abby smiled at him, "I am now. That was quite the ride though."

The pair, who had finally recovered from their harrowing escape, had ridden back to where Harley had dropped his trailer, hooked it to the rear of the Road Glide, and found a place down the street to stop and find some nourishment. Searching for Atlantis and being chased by a killer tsunami tends to increase one's appetite. They devoured their meal with hardly a word between them. Now as they waited for dessert and observed the news report, both were somewhat subdued over the final words from the announcer.

"Do you suppose everyone got out of the Jamestown and Roanoke areas?" Abby asked.

"I hope so. I mean, after all, they had plenty of notice to evacuate the low-lying areas. Just the thought of the two amulets and all the other stuff we found being lost is depressing, though."

"Yeah, I know you must be feeling down about that, but Harley," she leaned over and lowered her voice, "you discovered the location of Atlantis!"

Harley grinned at that thought. "It's crazy, isn't it?" He took a deep breath. "I just wish my mom could have seen this."

"I'm sure she's very proud of you. On another note, could you explain why you thought that the early colonists were splitting up the amulets, as opposed to just keeping them safe?"

"Do you remember John Smith's note to Christopher Newport?"

"Yeah."

"Well, if you think about it, he mentioned that he was splitting up the amulets, which didn't really make any sense if they needed them to find Atlantis. It would make sense to keep them together. Second, Smith mentioned getting revenge if he died. If Smith and Newport knew the amulets were cursed, and wanted to get rid of the others who had attempted to kill Smith, what better way than to reunite the amulets and let nature take its course, so to speak. We saw, firsthand, what happened when the pieces were brought together. Complete and utter destruction, just like you said."

Abby was quietly listening to Harley's explanation, nodding in agreement as he worked through the process. "Anything else?"

"Well, Smith said they could continue with their endeavor, and it doesn't make any sense that splitting all of the amulets up would help them in any way, shape, or form to *find* Atlantis. Finding Atlantis would involve a return to Roanoke, not a trip to Plymouth, which is in the opposite direction."

"Wow! *You* figured that out all by yourself? I guess you are smarter than you look?" Abby teased.

"I already told you that I'm a genius. I got you, after all." Harley ribbed.

Abby sighed. "I suppose I'll keep you." Then she frowned.

"What's wrong?" Harley asked, noting her change of expression.

"Nothing really, but I was just wondering who we should tell about our discovery."

Harley had a look of absolute trepidation. "Abby, we can *never* tell anyone. You do understand, don't you? Think of the danger. Just because the clues were destroyed does not mean that anyone who pursued it wouldn't be in harm's way. We need to be like the early colonists. We need to let it go."

Abby smiled, "Good, I was hoping you would say that."

Harley reiterated, "Abby, no one, okay? Not ever. I thought I was doing the right thing by keeping you out of this, and I still nearly got you killed. I don't want either of us ever to be responsible for anyone else's death."

The intensity in Harley's voice shook Abby to her core, causing her to shudder. "You're right, Harley, never. I promise. We both have lost enough."

Harley sat back, relieved. "I'm sorry," he said quietly, "I didn't mean to scare you." He recalled what he had said and done the previous year. "I don't want to hurt you ever again. Abby, will you forgive me for what I did and said last year?"

"I already did, the minute you said 'we' back there on the beach. Even before you explained it all to me, I knew there had to be a logical reason, and that one word told me you still thought of us as a team. That's all I needed to know. So yes, I forgive you. Do you forgive me?"

"For what?"

Abby reddened. "I used some really foul language right after you left. Grandma Larson about had a coronary when she heard me." By now Abby was crimson.

Harley could barely suppress his laughter. "Not very lady-like," he mocked.

"I never said I was a lady, but I think Grandma thinks I should be."

Harley squeezed her hand. "The last thing I want in my life is some uptight, prissy female. My girl rides motorcycles, stares down tsunamis, and saves lost puppies." He whimpered for her benefit.

"Darn tootin'" Abby replied.

"Oh, and by the way, I forgive you too."

Abby gave Harley her most alluring smile. Nearly hypnotized, he had to shake his head to come out of the Abby-induced trance.

"What?" Abby purred demurely.

"Let's go," he said abruptly.

"Where?" Abby questioned.

"Virginia. I need to say goodbye to our friend Chris. Then I need to get you safe and sound back home to Grandma Larson, so she knows you're really okay."

"And then...?" Abby's voice lingered, hoping. She didn't have to wait long. Fulfillment would finally come to her as well.

"Then we need to start our lives together, you and me."

Epilogue

20 Years Later

THE TWO MOTORCYCLES pulled slowly into the parking lot at the Fort Raleigh National Historic Site, the location of the Lost Colony of Roanoke. The bikes pulled to a stop, and the riders shut down the rumbling engines. Dismounting, a handsome man in his late 30s assisted a little boy of about 10 or 11 from the backseat of his jet black machine. Likewise, a beautiful woman, about the same age as the man, reached behind her own seat and helped a little girl of about 7 or 8 dismount from a pearl blue Harley-Davidson.

"Did you like the ride here from the campground?" the mother asked the little girl.

"Uh-huh, but I'm glad we didn't have to ride all the way from home. That would be too long."

Her mother grinned and called over to her husband. "Did you hear that? Good thing you bought that bike trailer or your little girl wouldn't have come along."

The man, who had removed his helmet, and was working on the strap of the boy's helmet, just smiled and nodded. "You don't mind riding, do you?" he asked the little boy."

"It's okay, Dad, but I'm glad we have the truck and trailer too."

That was not the answer the man was expecting. "Guess we'll have to toughen up your butts," he teased.

"I'd say these two are pretty tough already. Not too many kids go cavorting all over the country, especially on the backs of two Harley-Davidsons." She gathered the youngsters to her and gave them a big hug.

"Cut it out, Mom!" the little boy protested.

"Are you too old for your mom to give you hugs and kisses?" the man asked.

"It's just embarrassing. That's all."

"Fine, more for me," and the man reached over and gave the woman a loud smack on the lips.

"Oooh, that's gross!" the two children cried.

162

"Okay, okay, we're done," the man said, laughing.

"You're done," the woman responded, "but I'm not." She reached up and grabbed the back of the man's head and pulled his face toward hers, kissing him passionately.

"Oooo! Stop it! We don't know you!" the boy complained.

The embrace lasted a few seconds longer, and as the man pulled away, he whispered, "You're still beautiful."

The woman never hesitated, "And you're still cute."

The boy cut in, "Why are we here?"

"A little history lesson for you two."

"Again?" the little girl complained. "Is that all you two ever do?"

The man laughed. "It runs in the family, honey. Grandma and Grandpa used to do the same thing. In fact, Grandpa took me to this very place on my first motorcycle trip."

The boy seemed more interested now. "You've been here before, Dad?"

The man hesitated. "A long time ago, when I was just a little older than you."

"So what is this place?" the boy asked.

"It's called the Lost Colony of Roanoke," the mother explained. "It was the first English colony in America."

The boy protested, "My teacher said Jamestown was!"

"First permanent settlement," the father corrected, "but this one was earlier. The people just disappeared, though, so we don't really know what exactly happened to them. That's why it is called the Lost Colony."

"Oh, I get it. Hey, Dad, wouldn't it be cool if we found something here that would solve the mystery?"

The man looked at the woman before he spoke. Their glances spoke volumes. "That would be something," he agreed finally.

"Can we go look around, Daddy?" the little girl asked.

"I don't know, *can* you?"

"Ugh! *May* we?"

"You may. Just don't wander off too far."

"Okay, Daddy. Come on, let's go," she cried happily, pulling her older brother's hand. Off the two ran.

"Been a long time, hasn't it?" the woman said quietly.

"A really long time," the man agreed. "It's been rebuilt since it was destroyed by that tsunami that hit Plymouth and Jamestown too. A lot of it looks the same, but it is definitely different."

They proceeded hand in hand around the park and through the trails, taking in the sights and enjoying the walk near the shore. Occasionally the kids would come running by, reassuring their parents that they were fine. On one of the passes, the little boy yelled, "Dad, may we go down by the beach?"

"That's fine, just stay out of the water. You don't have your suits on. We'll be right behind you."

The two children raced toward the beach.

"Anna, you stay by your brother," her mother called. "Christian David, you watch your sister."

"I will, Mom. You don't have to use my middle name, you know. I haven't done anything wrong."

"Not yet, anyway," his mother laughed. "Now go have some fun."

The parents strolled peacefully along the shore, while the children raced along the shore, searching for seashells and whatever else might have washed up on shore.

After a few minutes, the little girl named Anna called out, "Mommy, Daddy, look what I found."

She was holding something in her hand. Her brother reached her first, noticed what she possessed, and immediately fell to his knees as if in search of something he might have dropped. Instead his hand thrust into the sand, and he held a fist up triumphantly. "I found one too!"

"What do you have there," his father asked, "a shell, or a new pet?"

"Neither," the boy shouted. "Anna found a really cool looking rock, and I found one too."

By now, the parents had reached the two excited children, and they quickly held out their hands to show their parents the treasures they had found.

"Mommy, mine looks like an O with a line through it," Anna exclaimed.

"Dad, mine sort of looks like the letter a. What do you think they are?" Christian asked simultaneously.

The children's parents looked startled at the sight of the small charms that the little boy and girl were holding. The boy said, "Is everything okay, Dad? You have a weird look on your face."

His father quickly recovered and said in the most indifferent way he could, "Oh, nothing Christian. It's just that they look very interesting."

"Can we keep them, Daddy?" little Anna asked.

Her mother cut in before he could reply. "Anna, do you know where we are?"

"North Carolina," was her innocent reply.

Her mother smiled at her, but she shook her head. "What I mean is that do you know we are on federal land?"

"I don't know what that means," Anna replied.

Anna's dad cut back in, "What your mother means, Anna, is that when we are at a place like this, we can't take things from it. How did you say it years ago, honey?"

"Take only pictures and leave only footprints."

"So you see, Anna, we can't take these with us."

"Aw, Dad, it's just two little stones!" Christian complained.

"I know, bud, I know, but it's the right thing to do," his father explained patiently.

"Oh, all right," the boy conceded. He stood up and dropped the small piece to the ground.

"You know what, Christian," his mother injected, "you two could at least have some fun with those two little stones. Why don't we try skipping them out into the water? Here, I'll grab one and so will Dad, and we'll all throw them at once, okay?"

"Good idea, honey," her husband replied. The adults reached down quickly and grabbed the first rock they could find.

"On three," their mother said, "1, 2, 3!" The entire family side-armed their projectiles out into the ocean, watching them skip, and then sink to the bottom.

"There, now," their father said, wiping the sand off his hands, "that was fun." He glanced at his wife, raised his eyebrows, and shook his head in disbelief. Her return look was one of absolute relief. He turned back to the children, "Do you want to keep skipping rocks?"

Christian, who was ready to reach for one, looked up suddenly, and pointed at the sky. "Uh, Dad, I think a storm is coming."

The adults spun around and peered at the sky. There were a couple of huge thunderheads in the sky. As the family of four peered at the sky, the clouds began to dissipate, being replaced with a brilliant blue sky. "You know what, kids, those do look like storm clouds, but you know what else?

"What?" they chorused.

Before he answered he reached over and grabbed his wife, pulled her to him, and then pulled the two children into a group hug. Finally he said, "Don't worry about any storms today. I think they will pass right over us this time. Don't you think so, honey?"

His wife reached up and gently kissed him on the lips. "You're right. We've seen the worst of it. It's going to turn out to be a beautiful, and fulfilling, day."

The End

CPSIA information can be obtained
at www.ICGtesting.com
Printed in the USA
FFOW04n0937101016
28336FF